ZARA

MARCUS HAMILTON

This book is for BreeMonks, my favourite person, best friend, and someone who will appreciate the blood and guts within ... as in within the book, but also within people, especially when they come out after that person has been peeled with a potato peeler.

Happy Birthday, BreeMonks. You are the best by so far it is hard to even see you up there.

Day 1

I'd never known anyone like her. None of us had. She arrived like the afternoon wind on a Summer day, cooling the heat that had held us captive. She touched us so gently at the start that we didn't even realise it was happening, and then, by the end, she was a presence none of us could ignore, a gale force, a whirlwind, tearing through us like we were paper.

She changed everything.

She changed everyone.

She changed me.

That first day, when she started at school, it was no different to any other new kid starting at any other new school.

At first.

She seemed shy, standing up the front as Mrs Brewer, our principal, introduced her to the class. Her name was Zara, transferring from another school, interstate, far away, another world.

Zara looked down as the information and requests of us continued, her shoulder-length hair falling forward over her face, and then, as the introduction finished, she looked up and smiled, and we all sucked in a breath. It was as though the air changed, the world changed.

Her eyes locked on us, round, innocent, somewhere between blue and grey, somewhere between nervousness and laughter. She captured us in that smile as though she was spreading joy through each and every one of us, and then, as suddenly as it had started, it disappeared, and she went to the seat that was waiting for her.

I can still see it now, even after everything.

The seat was two across and one down from me, far enough away that I couldn't make out every detail like I wanted to, close enough so that when she turned to sit, her scent reached me, a perfume that smelt like pastel blues and greys.

They would become the colours I associated with her,

always, the colours that always remind me of her.

Mrs Brewer left, her duties carried out, Mr Gallagher started teaching, and everything snapped back to normal, in a heartbeat.

She touched us so gently at the start that we didn't realise it was even happening.

By the end, she was a presence none of us could ignore, a gale force, a whirlwind, tearing through us like we were paper.

She changed everything.

She changed everyone.

She changed me.

And things would never return to how they had been before.

Day 3

On day 3, people noticed the breeze. They noticed its touch, gentle and sweet. They noticed the pastel blues and greys, the swirl of the black scarf around her neck, despite the warmth of the day. They noticed the smile. They noticed the strand of hair that crossed her forehead.

They noticed everything.

Because it was impossible not to.

She moved like liquid, flowing around the room, swirling to her chair, settling, gentle waves, ripples, a perfectly still lake.

When Mr Osborne asked for an answer to a calculus question, her hand went up immediately. Her response, which was correct, brought forth ripples and murmurs, breaking the surface tension. Zara looked around, smiling, not looking for acceptance or acknowledgment, just smiling at everyone, letting them know they were in her world.

Not everyone.

Almost everyone.

Pastel blue and grey with every turn.

Not everyone smiled back.

She was different.

Not restrained.

Not in her box.

The ripples eased and came to rest.

Mr Osborne moved on.

As he wrote on the whiteboard, she turned to the one person she'd missed on her smiling lap of the room, and she flashed, for an instant, a smile that rocked the world.

A smile to the one person she'd missed.

A smile to me.

Her eyebrow raised slightly, a tiny movement, enough for me to notice, then it dropped again, and she turned back to look at Mr Osborne, concentrating, learning, absorbing.

I realised later that was what she did. She absorbed. She absorbed everything, and that, in the end, was the reason things went the way they did.

It was what made her who she was, and it was what broke her.

Day 7

It was only day 7.

The cracks hadn't even started to appear, in her or in our world.

Nothing was broken.

The breeze was still gentle, twisting and turning to her chair, not bothering anyone else, but becoming a part of their day.

Part of the routine.

Except she was anything but routine.

She wore clothes that weren't quite in style, in time, but weren't right out there either, and although her outfit changed, she wore the same scarf every day, her neck always covered. I pictured that neck, in my mind, over and over, every time slightly different from the time before, every time the perfect neck.

Other people started to talk about it, wondering why she

wore it, and they made up stories.

I heard some of them, the stories, but I ignored them. I couldn't have cared less why she wore the scarf, why it was there, what the meaning was, if any.

She wore the scarf.

That was enough for me.

I only cared that she was there, and that each day, when she flowed into the room, I was already seated, so she had to look at me as she went to her chair.

I didn't even know this girl!

The only time I had heard her speak was when she answered questions in class. She hadn't yet made friends, and sat on her own at lunchtime. I watched her when I wasn't playing cards or going outside.

Or even when I was.

She would sit, on her own, and she would read.

A new book each day.

At the end of lunch, she would get up and leave, and the book would be there, waiting for someone to take it.

At first, no one did.

I didn't even know if she had finished it when she left.

I wanted to know.

I was even starting to want to know about the scarf.

I wanted to know everything.

I was fascinated by her.

She was a mystery, seeping into my consciousness, but she was smoke, wind, mist, there was nothing I could grab on to.

'You should speak to her.'

I'd said it to myself, a thousand times already, and now Glenn was saying it as well.

'You watch her every lunchtime, stalker. What, do you feel sorry for her?'

I shook my head, and it was true. I didn't feel sorry for her at all, in fact I felt jealous of her. She would sit, alone, reading, and her face told me, told everyone, if they looked, the story.

It showed what she was reading.

It dug deep into the souls of the characters and brought them to life with a movement of her eyebrows or a twitch of her mouth into that crooked smile.

Or she would laugh out loud.

She would actually laugh out loud.

At a book!

Of all things!

I didn't know how she did it but I wanted to be in it, to be drawn into a world like that, to be able to feel the words as they seeped into my mind.

I didn't feel words like that.

'I'm not going to speak to her. Not yet. Maybe in class, if she needs help.'

Glenn laughed.

'Have you heard her in there? I don't think she needs any help. And like you would talk in class anyway.'

I smiled.

It was true.

I didn't know what school she'd come from, but she knew things I had never even heard about.

'I'll speak to her one day,' I said. 'Now come on, deal.'

Glenn laughed and we returned to our card game, others joining us as lunch went on. I didn't look at her again, not directly, but I stole a glance with a card dropped to the ground, when I took my lunch wrapper to the bin.

I stole a glance and went back to my game a different person.

Lighter somehow.

The bell went and I headed to class.

We had electives.

She closed her book with a sigh, rested it on the seat with a gentle stroke, and got up, walking to her class, different to mine, but our paths had to cross. Glenn gave me a tiny shove, a little increase in pace, subtle, but enough to ensure I would reach the same point as her at the same time.

I waved my hand behind me, waving him off, but still I walked at the pace I needed to.

Our paths crossed.

We both stopped, waiting for the other one to go, both being the polite one.

'It seems,' she said, crooked smile, 'that we are at an impasse.'

I nodded. I wouldn't have even known what impasse meant if I hadn't watched movies. No one spoke like that in real life.

But she wasn't real life.

This wasn't real life.

This was here and now and nothing else mattered.

And it was only day 7.

Day 9

On day 9, I spoke to her. They were the first words I said to her, and I regretted them almost immediately.

It was at lunch, again, and we were playing cards, again, and I was watching her, again.

She had a different book, of course, but the others were still there, on the seat next to her.

People hadn't started taking them yet.

She had on a different outfit, of course, was wearing a hat and, as always, the same black scarf curled around her neck, holding on like it needed her, like it couldn't let go, even if she had wanted it to.

I needed to know.

I needed to see her neck, to be allowed into her world like no one else.

I went to the bin to throw out my lunch wrapper, and on my return she saw me watching her, and she smiled.

Not crooked smile, this was full smile.

Almost world-rocking caliber.

'Impasse,' she said, 'is a wonderful word.'

I nodded again. Three million things to say raced through my head, and any one of them would have been better than the one I "decided" on.

The one that came blurting out.

'Why do you wear that scarf every day? And why is it black?'

The smile disappeared.

The eyes closed slightly, as if looking into me.

As if upset with me.

And then the smile returned.

'You noticed I'm wearing a scarf? Oh, happy day!'

And then she posed, stroking the scarf, her hands showcasing it for me, for everyone who was watching, and it felt like *everyone* was watching.

Three million things to say raced through my head, and any one of them would have been better than the one I "decided" on.

Because I said nothing at all.

She stood and leaned in close, her lips near my ear, her hair brushing my face, all my senses a swirl of pastel blues and greys, my soul screaming at me, "You're alive now!".

'It's charcoal,' she whispered. 'But black was a good guess.'

Then she moved away, laughing, reaching inside and grabbing all of me with a world-rocking smile.

I stared, searching my everything for something to respond with, but in the end I simply turned and walked away, heading to my locker, needing to get away, needing to understand what she was doing to me, why I was acting this way, why my brain was betraying me.

Why my body was betraying me.

Once, before Avril, I could speak to anyone.

Things had changed since then, but this was on a whole different level.

I didn't speak as much.

Not anymore.

And definitely not her.

What was she doing to me?

As I opened my locker, turning the combination, I knew exactly what she was doing to me.

She was being herself.

And that was all she ever needed to do for me to be hers.

Day 10

The next day, I felt more confident.

'Nice scarf,' I said as I went by her, not mocking, gently teasing, and not stopping this time, simply speaking as I walked, and then turning and looking back, worried about what I would see, my heart leaping when I saw the crooked smile.

She nodded at me, and went back to her book.

I looked away from her face and, for the first time, I saw an empty seat next to her.

The books were gone.

She was starting to touch people, making them curious, brushing by them, letting them feel the change in the air.

I could feel it.

I had seen her.

And my smile couldn't have been wider.

Day 13

The weekend came and went. I thought about her the entire time, wondering where she lived, what she was doing.

I sat at my table before school started on Monday, waiting, drumming my fingers, eyes never leaving the door except when my arm was itchy, and I looked down to scratch it.

And that, of course, was when she arrived.

'Nice shirt,' she said as she weaved through the tables,

taking the long way to her seat, walking behind me in a flash of fluid movement, in a whisper of the wind.

My head spun up and around in shock, but she was gone, dissolving into her chair, smiling and saying good morning to the people around her, whether they responded or not, and it was mostly not, and I watched her, my eyes almost as wide as hers, if that were possible.

Which it wasn't.

She turned and looked at me, coyly, crooked smile, eyes sparkling blue, my heart not leaping but pounding, racing, bursting, full.

Blood flowed like whitewater through my veins, my heart giving them life, her giving me everything else.

'Oh boo,' Julie said, breaking the moment, breaking the connection.

I spun around.

Julie.

Always Julie.

If she wasn't the centre of the world, then the world had to stop.

I looked back. Zara was already in her book, reading, ignoring Julie, waiting for class to start.

The bell went.

Mr Gallagher came in.

Glenn punched my shoulder and laughed at me, and life was back to normal again.

Only it wasn't.

It never would be, never could be.

I punched him back and focused on school, stealing a glance at her every now and then, needing to see her, needing more of her, needing to speak to her, just her and me, no one else around, just us, no one else.

Then I would find out about everything.

I would find out about her.

I'd never seen or known anyone like her, and I knew I

never would again.

I would delve into her and I would never come out.

Back then, at Day 13, I didn't know how true that would be, and I didn't know what it would actually mean for that to happen.

And part of me wishes it never had.

Day 20

It was only day 20, and yet she had infiltrated every cell of my being. Of all our beings. At least, that's what I thought. But then again, she was all I thought about. They say you love someone when they are the last thing you think about at night and the first thing you think about in the morning.

Well I did that, and more.

She was on a continual loop, swirling and flowing through my mind and my spirit, holding me in, twisting around me, lifting me up.

I thought about her all day, and when the thoughts of her didn't keep me awake, she was in my dreams, haunting me.

Taunting me.

Creating me.

Every day now, the book would be gone. Taken almost as soon as it was left.

She was touching people.

She was changing the entire school.

People were reading, discussing books.

A book club started up.

She was in it, of course, and I was too.

Of course.

I would go, and I wouldn't talk, I would just watch as she described how she felt about a book, and like me, everyone would be mesmerised.

On Day 20, I looked for ways to talk to her, any way at all. I asked her for a pencil during class, walking past three people to get to her.

She gave me a pencil.

I went up to her at lunch and asked her what she was reading, despite the fact that she was holding the book out in front of her, so anyone could see what it was.

Stargirl.

It was obviously Stargirl.

But I asked her what it was anyway.

I needed an in.

I needed her.

She humoured me.

'Stargirl,' she said. 'By Jerry Spinelli. You should read it. Be quick though, there's a bit of a race for the books at the end of lunch these days.'

She smiled, pleased about that, then she motioned for me to lean in, and when I did, she lifted her body slightly and whispered.

'Take it now. I want you to read it with candles burning. It will transform you.'

She closed it, stroked the cover gently, then held it out.

I took it, my finger touching hers, the barest of touches, the strongest of surges.

There was a pause.

'*You* haven't got a candle.'

Blurted out.

Painfully.

Embarrassingly.

I tried again.

'Obviously.'

There was no verbal response, only a slight smile, her hand playing with the end of her scarf, and those round, innocent eyes narrowed slightly, looking inside me again, reaching into me and twisting everything upside down.

She didn't need a candle.

Obviously.

She was already transformed.

I smiled back, a forced smile, and then I turned and went to play cards, feeling her watching me, feeling everyone watching me.

I couldn't have cared less.

Watch me, I wanted to cry. All of you, watch *me* all you like, because then you aren't watching her.

But I knew they would turn back soon enough, back to her, to their own questions.

And so would I, even before I got to the card table.

She was hypnotic and she was mesmerising, and there would have been a time when I knew the difference between those two words, and now I didn't care.

I cared about one thing, and one thing alone.

And it was only Day 20.

Day 21

I hadn't slept again.

Not enough, anyway.

I had stayed up late, reading Stargirl, a candle burning, vanilla scented, and then I had turned out the light.

But I didn't sleep.

I lay awake, staring into the darkness, thinking about her, about the things I could say to her.

I lay awake, staring into the darkness, and I felt sick in my stomach at the things I had already said.

I replayed those conversations, only this time I was smoother, smarter, less obviously bashing past people to get a pencil.

And she responded.

She spoke to me in her voice, low, edged with huskiness, her eyes locked on mine, her perfect lips forming perfect words, perfect shapes.

I could see her in front of me, in the room, sitting on the

edge of the bed as we spoke again, this time in a real conversation.

I had all those thoughts, and then it was Day 23, and on Day 23, everything changed.

It went from two bubbles - her in one, everyone else in the other - to one bubble.

Us.

There may have been another bubble, other bubbles.

I didn't care.

I cared about our bubble.

I was drowning in her, floating, melting, anything to do with water and bliss I was doing it.

I walked straight past Glenn and the others at lunch and went and sat next to her.

I put my vanilla candle between us, I lit it, I opened Stargirl, and I began to read.

I heard a laugh from somewhere.

I ignored it.

We didn't speak a word for the entire lunch.

We just sat.

I read Stargirl, she read Wonder.

New day, new book, new life.

The candle went out, and I didn't even notice.

But I did notice, out of the corner of my eye, her fingernails painted blue and grey, sliding up and down, a book more for her than just words on a page, it was a full experience, emotional, physical, sight, touch, heart.

I noticed her knee touch mine, for a millisecond, like our fingers had, and then move away, and I noticed the chill of warm ice it sent through my entire body.

But it wasn't enough. I wanted to talk to her alone, just her and me, no one else around, just us, no one else.

After a time, I noticed myself turn to look at her, which was when I realised she wasn't reading anymore, she was watching me, staring at me, smiling at me.

Then her face turned serious, and the warm ice sent

goosebumps over my skin.

'We need to talk,' she said, 'alone, just you and me, no one else around, just us, no one else.'

I nodded.

She was in my brain.

She knew my thoughts, she knew everything about me, and I knew nothing about her.

'This afternoon would be good,' she said, 'but I have tuba practice. So tomorrow then. After school. You know where, right?'

I nodded again, and it was only when she slapped my knee, got up and left, it was only as I watched her go, that I realised I had absolutely no idea where "where" even was.

But I also realised it didn't matter.

I would know.

I would find her.

How could I not?

Day 23 - School

'So it's all about her now?' Glenn asked. 'What, we're not friends anymore?'

He'd grabbed my top as I'd walked past the card table again, to go and sit with her, be part of her. I stopped and shook my head. Explaining an other-worldly feeling wasn't easy.

'Of course we're friends,' I got out. 'We're always friends. We've been friends since we were 5.'

Glenn stared at me.

'Do you remember Avril Matthews?' he asked.

I turned away. She was watching us. He was going there.

'Yeah, of course you do,' he continued. 'How could you forget?'

I turned back.

'Don't,' I said. 'Why would you bring her up again? This isn't like that. It won't be like that. This isn't like anything. You can't understand.'

'Dude, this is Avril all over again (*It wasn't*). Avril in a handbasket. I just hope for your sake it doesn't end like that did (*It didn't. I wish it had*).'

He let go of my shirt and went and sat down.

'We'll be here playing if you want to join us,' he said.

My breath came out slowly, and I closed my eyes. When I opened them I turned to look at her, but all I saw was a book lying on the seat.

I looked everywhere, but she was gone.

I went over and picked up the book.

Pan's Whisper.

I stroked the cover, relishing the smoothness of it, the thought that only a moment before she had been touching it, blue and grey nails sliding up and down the side.

I held the book to me for an instant and then I went and played cards, smiling at the teasing that came my way, joining in the fun, physically there, every other part of me already done with school, going to the "where" that she would be, just her and me, just us, no one else.

Last period passed slowly. Slower than ever. Time seemed to go backwards.

She didn't seem to notice.

She sat at her desk, working, answering questions with a smile, glancing round the room every now and again, letting everyone know she was there, that they were in her world.

They knew.

On Day 24, at school, there was a change.

A change in the air, in the feel of … of everything.

The breeze strengthened.

The water, which had been glass, started to move.

Small waves formed.

Some kids don't like other kids who know everything.

Some kids don't like other kids who think they're better.

Some kids don't like other kids whose clothes don't quite match.

Some kids don't like other kids who show off.

She's *not!* I wanted to shout. This *isn't* showing off! She knows the answer and so she says it, simple as that.

She wouldn't know how to show off.

She's just her.

She answered another question.

Little white peaks on the tips of waves.

'Jeez, wanna give someone else a go?'

I spun my head around.

Julie.

Always Julie.

She had been the smartest, the prettiest, the nastiest for a long time now.

She was still one of those three things.

She could never be the other two.

Not now.

White peaks, foaming, crashing.

Zara turned to Julie, that crooked smile on her lips, her eyes still sparkling, wide, round, but not the same.

More grey than blue now.

Like the sky over the churning water.

'I'm so sorry,' she said, her voice genuine, no sarcasm, not like we usually heard in an apology. 'I just knew it so I put my hand up. That's all.'

Julie sneered, contrasting the crooked smile.

'Yeah, well what you have to know is that we don't like people who -'

'That's enough, Julie,' Mr Gallagher said 'If you know the answer, you're welcome to put your hand up. Would you like to answer the next question?'

Julie nodded and smiled, then glanced at Zara and her eyes went hard.

Dark clouds.

Julie whispered something to Ashleigh, sitting next to her, and they giggled.

Mr Gallagher asked the question.

Ashleigh started drawing something.

Julie didn't know the answer.

Mr Gallagher turned to the board and started writing out the question, asking if anyone else knew the answer as he wrote. Ashleigh showed Julie what she'd drawn and they laughed.

No one had said anything, and so Mr Gallagher asked again.

No one knew the answer.

Almost no one.

Zara put her hand up, slowly, looking around the room as she did, seeing if anyone else was going to go.

They weren't.

They didn't.

All eyes were on her.

The note was being passed around to giggles and smirks, stares, fingers pointing.

'Don't,' Julie whispered. 'Don't answer.'

Zara's hand continued to rise, inch by slow inch.

The note was getting nearer to me.

I didn't want to see it.

Her eyes fell on me.

The note fell on my desk.

Her eyes drifted to it and then back to me.

I shook my head at her.

Don't change for them, I thought. You answer whatever you want to answer.

Be *you*.

There is *no one* like you.

Her hand stopped rising.

A harsh wind blew, stirring the waves.

She looked at the note again, then at me, and tilted an eyebrow.

Mr Gallagher wasn't looking, but now he'd almost finished writing.

Soon he would turn.

He would see her hand.

I opened the note and looked at it, a picture of her with her brains oozing out of her head, zombie-style, and a little speech bubble saying, "I'm so smart!"

It was basic, like Ashleigh. I crumpled it up and threw it at the bin.

I missed.

Ashleigh and Julie laughed, and so did their friends, and Ashleigh went to pick it up, bumping me on the way past.

I turned back to Zara. She was staring at me, her eyes changed now, light blue, curious, inquisitive.

Answer it, I thought. Forget about Julie. She doesn't matter. You matter. Only you. Show them how smart you are. Smart is sexy. Let *them* get smarter to beat *you*, don't let them change you.

Don't go down to their small-town level.

Don't.

Now her hand slowly lowered, her eyes still on me, every other set of eyes in the room, save Mr Gallagher's, on her. She raised her eyebrows for an instant and flashed me a full smile, her eyes suddenly the brightest blue, and then her hand rested on her desk and she faced the front.

'Ha!'

Julie.

A laugh, more a bark, short, sharp and loud.

She thought she'd won.

Ashleigh dropped the note on Zara's desk.

She picked it up and put it in her pocket without looking at it.

Mr Gallagher finished writing and turned, just as Ashleigh sat down, the perfect crime.

'Anyone else?' Mr Gallagher asked as he faced the room, but really only facing her, his face shocked when he saw her there, hands on her desk, face impassive.

'No one?'

'No,' she said. 'Not this time, Mr Gallagher. This one I will have to research. Gosh, it's so tricky. I'll let you know tomorrow if I find the answer, unless you want to tell everyone now?'

He glanced quickly around the room, trying to work out if this was a joke.

It wasn't.

He smiled and said he would tell everyone now.

He knew what she was doing.

So did I, and I didn't like it.

She didn't need to hide how good she was.

Not from or for anyone.

She knew the answer.

Everyone knew she knew the answer.

Mr Gallagher went on with the lesson. The clouds blew away, and patches of blue shone through.

Archie, Julie's boyfriend, all-round sporto and idiot, threw a screwed-up bit of paper at Zara. It hit her shoulder and bounced off.

She picked it up and, once again, put it in her pocket without looking at it, and then lowered her eyes to her desk.

He threw another one, at me this time. I picked it up and threw it back.

I didn't have her control.

I watched her, willing her to look at me, willing her to understand my telepathic message that I was here for her, that I wanted her to be smart, that I wanted her to be amazing.

But she didn't look up.

The water would never be smooth again.

Day 23 – After school

'You're not like the other girls. Or boys. You're not like anyone.'

I had found "where." I had been walking, guessing, and suddenly she was there, with me, running up from behind.

She had chosen the perfect place, sitting outside

McDonalds in the carpark.

It was where everyone used to go, "used to" being the operative words.

The proud, upstanding citizens thought it didn't look nice to have teenagers outside the McDonalds, sitting and talking, so they put in a complaint.

McDonalds and the council discussed tactics and in the end came up with one that sent the teenagers scrambling, never to return.

They played classical music.

'This is Beethoven,' she said, ignoring my statement but answering it in everything she did, speaking partly to me, partly to herself, and partly to no one.

Beethoven.

'You know,' I said, shaking my head and smiling.

'Of course I do!'

Of course she did.

I loved that she knew.

Her voice lit up and, when I looked at her, I saw her eyes had lit up as well, bluer than ever, shining, swallowing me whole.

'See, Beethoven was deaf,' she said. 'He used to rest his head on the piano, feel the vibrations. He lost the one thing you would assume a great composer needed, and he still wrote … this!'

She waved her hand into the air in front of her, then she stared into the distance, like she could see the music.

It wouldn't have surprised me if she could have.

Nothing would have surprised me about her.

And it was only Day 23.

Not even four weeks.

She talked more about Beethoven, and I listened, but mostly I watched. They say communication is 7% words, that the rest is tone and inflection and pace and body language and everything else.

With her I couldn't work it out.

While her body was amazing and expressive, her face told a story of its own, her hands, arms, legs, chest, every part of her speaking, and she was loud and then quiet and thundering and then calm, but her actual words drew me in as well. The way she strung them together, the way she used words I never would have thought to use, and yet they worked.

It was like listening to a song, and I felt my body moving with hers, my face changing with hers, my smile matching hers.

She was light.

She was energy.

She was music.

She was Beethoven's finest symphony.

And he would never know.

Eventually she sat, next to me, her leg by mine, out of breath, panting, and I could hear the smile in her breath.

She reached down and took my hand, lifting it up in front of us.

'I could hold this hand,' she said. 'For a long time, I could hold it.'

Then she let it go and laughed, and went to swinging her legs in front of her. I stared at my hand, her touch lingering. Despite the dancing, despite the energy and the way she had flung her arms around, her hand had matched the cool air. I could feel the chill seeping into me, and wondered if she could feel my warmth seeping into her.

I couldn't take my eyes off my hand, off her hands.

'You don't have great circulation,' I said.

Her words were a symphony. Mine were barely a clunkily-played note.

She nodded.

'It's a burden I must carry,' she said, her hand rising to her forehead dramatically.

I laughed, and my heart swirled.

Bay of fools.

'Did you look at the notes?' I asked.

She didn't answer.

She stared at me for what seemed like forever, and I stared back, trying to count the colours in her eyes.

Her stare took everything out of me, holding it, changing it, and then giving it back.

But she didn't answer.

I tried a different tact.

'Why am I here?' I asked. 'Why me?'

A smile was added to the stare.

'Because you screwed up the note. You stood up for me even though you knew it would come at a cost. Because you were desperate to know more about me. Because you want me to be amazingly me. Because I knew that you would be the one who would help me. I *am* going to need help, Hunter. In time, I will need your help. Not now. In time.'

Although the smile stayed as she spoke, I could sense a change. Her eyes were still blue, but they had dulled slightly, as the greyness closed in.

I looked away, playing with my hands, wanting to tell her she didn't seem like someone who would need help, wanting to know what she would need help with, what she would want me to do, but I couldn't ask, thinking, thinking, until her hand found mine again, closing over it, stopping the fidgeting, stopping my heart.

I didn't say anything.

It felt as if for me to speak, right then, would break the spell.

I didn't want to break the spell.

She would tell me soon enough.

And when she did, I knew I would do whatever she wanted me to.

At least, that was what I thought then.

Day 24

Friday. The last day of the week. The last time I would see her for two days.

It felt like forever.

It still amazes me now, the connection we developed in such a short amount of time. The way we clicked, the way I felt like she knew me better than anyone ever had.

She knew me.

We had spoken more on Day 23, after the "needing help" silence. We had spoken for an age, and I found in myself an urge to give more to her than I had to anyone, even Glenn.

In an hour, she knew more about me than anyone else in the world.

In two hours, she knew nearly everything.

Because I gave her nearly everything.

It felt right.

She had unlocked me, somehow opening up the valve I had closed off, only opening every now and again, and then only slightly.

Now it was fully open.

Whatever she was doing to me scared me, but at the same time I liked it, and I didn't want it to ever stop.

But it did.

It had to.

We had walked from McDonalds, walking slowly, our arms brushing against each other often, my hand brushing her hip once.

I ached to kiss her goodbye, but when the time came, when we stood outside my house, I simply stared at her.

I froze.

She smiled her crooked smile, moved in, and hugged me, tight, close, a tiny noise escaping her as she did.

She felt real.

Solid.

Perfect.

The hug finished and I went to the door, stopping there

to watch her walk away, swinging her arms, swinging her hips, singing a low song as she went.

'Goodbye, Hunter,' she called. 'You can go inside now. I'm not that interesting to watch.'

I laughed.

She most certainly was, but I went inside anyway.

And when I went to bed, I slept.

And I dreamt.

And now it was Friday, and I only had one class with her, maths, in the morning.

That was it.

I would see her at lunch, or so I thought, and then I would have to wait until Monday.

We hadn't seen each other on any weekend before, and we hadn't mentioned anything of this coming weekend, if we would see each other, or if we would wait, so I was assuming we would wait.

And the wait increased, because at lunch, she wasn't there.

The seat was empty.

There wasn't even a book.

I scanned the room.

Maybe she was sitting somewhere else.

Maybe she was … where was she?

I started to panic.

Something was wrong.

It had to be or why wouldn't she be there?

A hand, on my shoulder, made me turn, and I could sense the disappointment in my own face, and I knew Glenn saw it too.

He smiled though.

'Sorry, man. Only me.'

I shrugged, forcing myself to look at him, and not to look for her.

'She left. Said she had to go. We were in art, and Julie and her had a … thing. Like a, I don't know, Julie had been saying stuff to her I couldn't hear, and then suddenly there was another note, she read it, went up and got a pass, and she was gone. I don't think she'll be back. Not today at least.'

I shrugged again, forcing myself to stay calm, only now realising that in all our talking we hadn't done anything about phone numbers.

Or addresses.

I couldn't check on her.

The only way we would see each other was at school.

On Monday.

A lifetime away.

Day 25

She was outside my house when I left to go to Glenn's. She sat, on the front lawn, cross-legged, eyes closed, meditating.

Waiting.

For me.

I stopped.

She didn't move.

Neither of us did, for an eternity, me staring at her, her staring into the darkness, the void of her closed eyes.

My mind was racing. What was she doing there? Why had she left school the day before? What was in the note? Was she okay? How had she found me? Where did she even live?

'It seems,' she said, her husky voice breaking the silence, shredding my thoughts, 'that we are at an impasse.'

I smiled.

So did she.

'I like your smile,' she said.

It disappeared.

'How did you …?'

My voice trailed off, into the void. She stood without using her hands, suddenly on her feet and in front of me, her eyes open and drawing me in, her face so close I could feel her breath, could smell her, feel her, making my skin tingle.

'I know everything,' she said mysteriously, her hand flashing between our faces, then lowering to show her smile. 'Plus,' she continued, moving away, 'how could you *not* smile? That was a great line. If you weren't smiling, I would have to reconsider my selection. I may start to think perhaps you're not the one.'

I *am* the one, I wanted to say. I wanted to hold her shoulders and tell her I was the one, and that I didn't know why, but I would do anything for her.

But I simply shrugged and smiled again, trying to be mysterious myself.

It didn't work.

She burst into laughter and hugged me.

So maybe it did work.

When she released the hug, she ran to my bike and started pedaling.

'Where are we going?' she asked as she rode away from me. I started running after her, sprinting to try and catch up.

'I was going to go to Glenn's,' I said. 'We kind of hang out every Saturday. But we can do something? Us?

'Nope, let's go to Glenn's. It's Saturday, and if that's what you do, that's what you do. But after that …'

She skidded to a stop, and I had to skip to the side to not crash into my own bike. Once I steadied, I realised she was staring at me, waiting to finish her sentence. I caught my breath and nodded.

'… after that you're mine, and we talk. You and me. I have some things I need to tell you, and some things I need to ask you, and some things that are not relevant to anything at all. Okay?'

I nodded.

'Okay.'

'Good. Now how the heck do we get to Glenn's?'

I laughed and started running, making her catch up this time.

Being at Glenn's was amazing. Do you know how, sometimes, you have something that you know is incredible, like the best thing in the entire world, and you just want to show it to everyone so they can see how incredible it is as well?

I do.

I know that.

And she didn't let me down.

She had Glenn hypnotised, mesmerised.

She had him mesmerised when she was speaking, and even when she was listening, because when she listened she gave you everything you needed.

Like me, he poured out his heart to her, telling her things even I didn't know, and it was as though he forgot I was even there when it was happening.

Or, if he remembered I was there, he didn't care.

I knew that feeling too.

She was amazing.

She became your world.

She absorbed everything.

When we left, she hugged Glenn and he watched us leave.

'Okay,' she said to me as we slowly went down the street. 'Your turn.'

My turn.

We sat on the swings at the park, not three blocks from my house.

We swung gently on them, barely moving and in opposite motion, her forward, me backward, her backward, me forward.

She watched her feet as she swung.

A strand of hair fell over her forehead.

That bothered me.

Because it distracted me.

It took everything not to reach out and stoke it away, and the only thing that helped me resist doing that was the fact it looked so beautiful.

'Who's Avril Matthews?' she suddenly asked, breaking the spell. I sucked in a breath.

How did she know everything?

'Avril Matthews,' I said.

Oh, Jesus.

Zara nodded, her eyes locked on mine, drawing me into her.

And the words came out.

Avril Matthews.

Eighth grade.

Avril Matthews had been my first girlfriend. I had loved her, or so I had told myself.

But whatever form of love it had been, it hadn't been enough.

It had to begin with, when I had ignored Glenn and my other friends, when I had spent all my time with Avril.

It had been enough when she had kissed me, my first kiss, and I had been smitten.

We had been happy.

And the mean kids, the cool kids, Julie, Archie, the others, they had known it.

And so they had torn it down.

They didn't have anything against us separately, as far as I knew, and as far as I could tell afterwards, but they hated us together.

Hated seeing us together, smiling, being us, not being the way they wanted us to be.

Not idolising them, lost in another world.

And so they had attacked her.

I don't know why they chose her, not me. Glenn said later it was because Julie liked me, but I didn't know if that was true, although now, with the beginnings of the same thing happening to Zara, I started to wonder.

I also knew they chose her, not me, because of Glenn. I wasn't big, at all, but Glenn was. Of all the kids, only Glenn escaped being picked on. He was big, and he knew how to fight, and it had got him in trouble more than once.

It had got him in trouble just last year for fixing up Archie when he was picking on some kid, and when Glenn stepped in, Archie took him on.

Archie didn't win.

But Glenn got in the most trouble.

Back then, with Avril, I didn't think about the why so much.

It didn't matter.

They had set about ruining her, her reputation, her friendships, her life.

And it had worked.

They had embarrassed her in front of everyone.

They had made up rumours about her.

They had stolen her friends.

They had cornered her behind the sheds, whispering to her, saying things no one else heard and no one else tried to hear.

At first, I had stood by her side, holding her as she cried, telling her I was there for her, that I would do anything for her.

But I hadn't.

I didn't.

She lost her friends, everyone backing away, until there was only me, and then it was just too hard, and I was a kid, scared of being torn down myself, scared that they would come for me next, and so I broke up with her.

I left her and she was left with no one, and they broke her down.

They broke her.

She broke.

And they all just watched it happen.

I just watched it happen.

I wanted to help, I thought about all the things I would do to help her, but all I did was think.

I was a face in the crowd, everyone and no one, and every

time she saw me, every time she silently pleaded with me to help her, to help her find the strength that she was losing, that she had carried with her for so long, every time she did that, I looked away, my mind racing, my heart racing.

And so there was no one there to build her back up again, we deserted her, hung her out to dry, and so she had left the school, left the town, but I had heard of her since, heard that she hadn't healed, couldn't heal, wouldn't heal.

As I spoke, as the story of Avril flowed out of me, I realised Zara was watching me intently, taking every morsel in, taking it all, and I realised I was crying, that the guilt I felt for letting Avril deal on her own was coming out, that Zara was making it come out, somehow, that talking to her about this was opening up old wounds, leaving them raw and real and bare and exposed, and that then there was a coolness, and she was healing me, and now I couldn't *stop* crying, because I had done *nothing!*

I had said I loved Avril, but then I had done nothing and I didn't know if I could live with that anymore except I could, I had to, because I was with her, and now she made me stand and she was holding me and whispering to me and I couldn't even understand the words, her charcoal scarf brushing against my cheek, her hands stroking the back of my head, and she was salve on my open wounds, stemming the flow of guilt blood, stitching me up, leaving the memory as a scar, one that I would run my fingers over now and again, never forgetting what had happened, but not feeling the pain as strongly anymore.

Not being infected by it.

Not holding on to it.

She saved me.

Who *was* she?

We stayed that way for a long time, just me and her, just us, in front of a gently moving swing, holding each other.

Eventually the tears stopped and I broke off the hug, embarrassed, not used to showing anything like that to anyone.

Not anymore.

I sat on the swing again.

She stayed standing, watching me.

'Sorry,' I said, moving my gaze to the ground.

A hand, a cool, soft, smooth hand, held my chin and raised my face, and I didn't know if it was the coolness of her skin or the lightness of her touch or the fact she was so close that gave me shivers.

Maybe it was all of the above.

She leaned in close, staring directly into my eyes, and I could see every tiny freckle on the bridge of her nose.

I gasped, catching it, too late.

It had happened.

'There will be a time for sorry,' she whispered, 'but isn't now. That was beautiful. That was everything to me. Never apologise for being real and raw, for showing me all of you. I need all of you, Hunter, and because of that, you will have all of me.'

She leaned in closer and kissed me then, her lips like her hands, so soft, so cool, those hands in my hair now, mine still holding to the swing chains, scared to do anything to break or change this moment.

This perfect moment.

The kiss deepened, and all I could taste was her, not just with my lips, but with my everything. The waves swirled and crashed but the sky was blue, the water was playing, jumping, leaping, and when the waves flattened out, when the kiss ended, to this day I don't know how I was still breathing.

She moved in and kissed me again, quickly, softly, and then she went to the bike and picked it up.

'Tomorrow,' she said, 'it's my turn. I have a lot I need to tell you, Hunter. A lot I need to ask you. Of you.'

I realised that was basically what she had said earlier, but I had ended up being the one doing all of the talking.

That had happened a lot.

She got on my bike and rode off. I didn't know if she expected me to follow her, to run alongside the bike like I had earlier, but I didn't.

I stayed in the swing, my hands still gripping the chains, and I closed my eyes and remembered how she had tasted.

Day 26

At 10 o'clock, when I went out the front door, she was waiting on the lawn again, my bike on its stand next to her. I didn't know how long she had been there, and I didn't ask.

It didn't matter.

If she'd just arrived, it was perfect timing.

If she'd been waiting for hours, she had been waiting for me.

Either way, she was there, and in the end that was all that mattered.

We didn't take the bike this time, we walked.

And walked.

And walked.

'Your story. Yesterday. Your story about Avril,' she said. 'It reminded me of a girl I knew. At one of my old schools.'

We'd been walking in silence for an hour. She broke the silence with that line. She broke the silence. Soon she would shatter the world.

'They picked on her. Teased her. Called her different. And she was, but they had never really bothered her. They kept their distance. It started off because of something silly, because she knew the answers, because she got a good result on a test.'

Her voice was different somehow. Quieter, yet deeper, more of a husk to it.

I could barely breathe as I listened to her, every word seemingly the key to everything.

'They teased her, called her names for being smart, but she laughed it off. She didn't mind. She was happy being her.'

I was waiting for the but.

'Then things turned. The names got nastier, the things they

said she'd done more untrue. They spread rumours, they played pranks, they found ways to humiliate her, destroy the things she loved. It even got physical one time, but nothing seemed to be able to get to her, not as far as they could see anyway.'

The but.

'I'm not telling you this to make you feel bad about not helping Avril Matthews, I know you're doing that to yourself anyway. I'm just telling you because …'

Her voice trailed off, and we walked in silence again.

When she spoke, her voice shook.

'I *know* you, Hunter. I feel the pain you feel. I couldn't help her. She was so brave, never letting them see what they were doing to her, but that only made it worse. That made them try harder. They were desperate to break her, desperate to bring her to her knees, and they never knew that she was already broken, that despite how it looked on the outside, every part of her inside was broken, bit by bit at first and then crumbling, a building smashed at the foundations.'

The but.

'She couldn't win. Not showing she was broken didn't work. If they knew they were breaking her, maybe they would have gone harder then too, driven by their success, wanting to finish her off.'

We had stopped walking, and I realised we were holding hands. I hadn't even noticed it happen, and yet we were, and our hands were wet with sweat, her nails digging into my knuckles.

'In the end they won. She couldn't take it anymore. She spoke up, told her parents, told teachers, and they did all they could to protect her but still the names, the rumours, the pushing, shoving, they took everything she was away from her, it kept coming, in secret, she couldn't go anywhere, she was so brave but it ripped all that she was apart, and she didn't know who she was anymore, didn't know how she should act, speak, walk, anything. She lost herself, and I lost her, and then she was gone, gone away, one day she just wasn't at school. They told us she had moved, that she was trying to start again. But I knew that wasn't true.'

The nails drew blood.

Blood froze in my veins.

It was as though I could feel every word she said. It was as though I was there, with her, desperate to help her friend, trying to help her friend, and being unable to do anything.

'She tried changing for them, you know. One time, when she was lost. She got lower grades, stopped answering questions, but it didn't matter. Not to them. They were on a roll and I don't think they could have stopped even if they'd wanted to. That's the thing, Hunter, by the end of it, I don't think even *they* knew what they were doing. They were in the whirlwind as much as she was. They'd dug this hole and they couldn't get out, so they had to keep digging.

It's like when you get a thrill, and it blows you away, but the next time the thrill is dulled, so you have to find something else, something more, and so you go harder. That was what they did, and every time, bits of her broke away, and every time, she lost more of who she was, until in the end, I don't think anyone knew who anyone was anymore. They were just things, beings, victim and torturer, heaven and hell, and there was nothing in between, and there was no God to save her.

And when she left, when she was gone, life went on. It was as though it had never happened. Tuesday came and went, and classes were taught. Wednesday, Thursday, and that was the worst of all, because it didn't just go on for her. It couldn't, because she didn't exist anymore, not really, not there, not at that school. She had been ruined. She had been ripped apart and broken down and no one had been able to put her back together again, and the rest of them just went on about their days.

I *tried*, Hunter. I know you feel you didn't with Avril, but I also know you would never do that again, that you wouldn't not try, that you would stand up, be there, that it isn't even always about facing up to the bullies, or making them stop, but that sometimes it's just about being there, listening, taking someone away from the world that they don't belong in, the world that is happy to chew them up, and taking them into a world where there is love and care and friendship and togetherness and laughter, and all those things become armour, they become protection, and it doesn't mean it's easier to get through, to be in it every day, but it does mean there's light, and no matter how thin the ray is, it's there and it's something to reach for, something to hold onto at night, when you're wondering if it's worth it, wondering if *anything* is worth it, wondering if *you* are worth it, that little ray of light, shining in, it isn't always enough, and sometimes it can't be grasped, and sometimes it gets blacked out, overcome by the darkness, but for an instant, sometimes, it can give hope.'

We'd stopped walking. I felt like I hadn't breathed in a lifetime. I felt like I never wanted to breathe again, not if it meant she stopped talking, not if it meant she stopped holding my hand, not if it meant I wasn't staring into those eyes, so grey now, a grey holding back the blue that longed to break out.

A grey of yearning and desperation.

I felt like I never wanted to breathe again if it meant never seeing that blue break free.

I didn't care about the nails, or the blood, or the pain, I didn't care about any of it. I cared about her, and I cared about her, and I cared about her.

'And do you know the worst thing? Hunter? Do you know the worst thing?'

There was more. There couldn't be more.

I shook my head.

'It happened more than once, Hunter. What I saw happen to her, I saw it again and again. I've moved around a lot, and every school I go to, it's the same story. There are bullies, and there are victims, and the bullies always win. Even when they get caught, even when they get punished, they still win, because the victim, and God I hate that word, it sounds pitiful and it isn't, because these kids, they aren't pitiful, they're wonderful and strong and beautiful and different, but this, this *shit*, it changes them. Every time it happens, a little bit of them dies and they are never fully them again. Never fully. And that is so sad it just makes me want to cry. All the time, it makes me want to cry.'

She loosened her grip and sighed, and the world turned again. A bird flew out of a tree, distracting me, and then we were walking, still holding hands, but the intensity was gone.

The story was finished.

I took her silence as a sign she was thinking about things, that she didn't want to be disturbed, that she had talked enough, that she was pushing it down, deep down, burying it, moving on.

If only I had been right.

Her thumb moved, the tiniest stroke, and right then, with that tiny movement, she threw away the key.

I was locked in, I was her prisoner.

I was in the whirlwind and I couldn't get out.

Day 27

It had started with Julie's "Oh boo" and "Wanna give someone else a go" comments.

Then the note, Archie throwing the paper.

If I look back, that was when it started.

That was the first crack.

That was when the wind strengthened.

The storm grew when the second crack appeared on Day 27.

27 days.

We hadn't even known her a month.

Long enough for her to change the world, our world, my world.

Long enough for Julie and her friends to decide they had a new target, someone to bring down a peg or two.

The second crack came with a test.

We had done it the week before, and I hadn't thought it important, but when we got it back, when she got hers, when she smiled, her eyes weren't blue like the ocean or the sky, but blue of purest joy, not a sliver of grey, and when she turned and showed it to me, pulling an oh-my-god-look-at-this-face then giving me a rock the world smile, giving me shivers that sent my entire body into goosebumps, that was when everything changed.

Silent thunder rocked the world like her smile had rocked mine.

Out of the corner of my eye I saw Julie whispering to Ashleigh who whispered to Sienna, and then Ashleigh looking at Zara, nodding and smiling.

Shivers again.

Of fear.

I wanted to yell out, to protect her, to warn her, but Mr Osborne was talking, telling everyone about the test results, how he had been pleased but how one student had stood out above all others, how one had scored a perfect 100.

I wanted to scream, Zara's story ringing in my ears. *Don't!* Don't bring attention to it, not now. She *knows!* She *knows* she smashed it. They'll turn on her. We all know it's her. It shouldn't matter that she's perfect, it shouldn't matter that you tell everyone how amazing she is, *I* want to tell everyone how amazing she is, but we can't, not right now, not when there's already a crack, not when the whirlwind is gathering. It shouldn't matter but it does. Don't do this to her, Mr Osborne, please, don't. I want you to, I want you to shout it from the rooftops, but the others, it will be all they need.

Don't let it start with a test result.

Not again.

Not like with that other girl.

Please don't let it.

I stared at her as he spoke. She was looking at her test, smiling, so proud, so happy.

She turned to me again and rocked my world, and I smiled back, my eyes telling her that I would be her ray of light. If things changed, if the crack widened, if anything happened, whatever they did, I would be her ray of light to hold onto when she lay down.

She could hold onto me.

Even if nothing happened.

Even if Mr Osborne said it and nothing happened, no one turned on her, I would still be her ray of light. I would shine on her every night, and I would hold her coolness in the warmth of my light, and I would protect her.

I just didn't know what to do, I didn't know how I could help, I couldn't, I couldn't speak.

But Mr Osborne could.

'I would like to tell you now, that student is -'

My hand shot up before I could stop it.

'Mr Osborne!'

Everyone gasped. Mr Osborne stopped talking. I felt her look at me. I felt everyone look at me. I didn't care. I was her ray of light. I wasn't letting this start. No way. Not her.

I took a breath, I swallowed, I looked at my desk and, for the first time in a long time, I asked a question in class.

'I was just wondering, with the test, I have some questions. Can you please explain some answers to me?'

'It's brilliant you are contributing, Hunter, but don't you think it can wait? I was in the middle of something.'

Giggles around the room. Heat rushing to my everywhere.

My hand was still straight up in the air, so I brought it down to my desk, and that was when I realised it was shaking. I put my other hand over it, trying to steady it, but I couldn't. I breathed in all of her, all of her courage, and I looked straight at Mr Osborne.

'I just think that what I'm going to ask will help other people too. I just think that it might be some things we all had trouble with.'

'Almost all,' he said, making me panic he was going to out her.

'Almost all.'

He sighed, then nodded, and leant against his desk.

I risked a glance at her.

She was looking at me, confused, her eyes a mixture of blue and grey, the hand that only the day before had been holding mine playing with her scarf, twisting it, stroking it.

'Hunter?'

I turned back to Mr Osborne, more giggles drifting around the room. Archie reached forward and pushed me, playfully enough to not get into trouble, hard enough to make me know I should have been quiet.

I asked my questions, brought up my concerns, made up my concerns, and Mr Osborne spent the rest of the class going over the test.

The crack closed over, the wind died down, the whirlwind came to rest.

For now.

Day 27 – After School

'Why did you do it? He had been going to say about the wonderful result someone got, whoever that may have been.'

I was walking home from school, alone, and then she was there, falling into step beside me, eyes sparkling.

I didn't look at her, the ground apparently intriguing.

My heart, still racing from jumping in and saving her, sped up even more with her there.

I didn't know what to say.

How could I say what I was feeling, what she was doing to me?

How could I say that I did it because I wanted to protect her, I wanted her to be okay?

How could I say that without making her seem weak, like someone who needed protecting?

How could I say it without making it obvious that I had fallen so hard and so deep for her that I didn't think I could ever get out?

How could I say that?

'I just, I had some questions,' I mumbled.

She laughed and pushed me, then danced in front of me, walking backwards, making me look at her.

I looked at her.

I couldn't not.

The ground lost all its intrigue that had never been there.

She was dancing as she moved backwards, her face alight, eyes alive, I could almost see the energy.

'Are all boys silly, or just you?' she asked me, laughter in her voice. I knew she wasn't mocking me, but I felt myself get defensive all the same.

'It's not just me. I had some questions.'

She sensed the change in my tone, and her energy changed too.

She stopped dancing.

She stopped moving backwards.

She stopped me with a hand on my chest.

Touch.

Life.

She moved in so her arm was bent, her hand still on my chest, her eyes staring directly into mine.

'I know why you did it,' she said, her voice low, husky. 'You were my knight in there, Hunter. You wanted to save me, protect me. Only you.'

Her hand, which had been resting lightly on my chest, moved over my heart and pressed a little harder.

'You lived here,' she said. 'You got out of yourself, out of your head, where you usually are, and you moved into your heart, and you did it for me. You were there for me. I knew it. I knew it so much. You're my ray of light.'

She was right. I did live in my head, overthinking, analysing, planning what I should do and then, when I finally decided, the moment had passed, and it was too late.

Not this time.

Her hand moved, slightly.

It felt as though lightning was passing through that hand into me, into my entire body.

I could almost hear the crackling of it, no, I *could* hear it, and I could *feel* it, coursing through my veins, making me feel alive, strong, hers, bonding me to her as the pressure her hand exerted increased even more, and I hadn't blinked, a micro second of not looking into her eyes too much to even bare thinking about.

And then she flashed a smile at me, kissed me on the lips, quickly, gave a little squeal of delight, and danced off, leaving me to watch her as she spun and twirled down the path, electricity crackling, my entire being tingling, my hand resting where hers had been.

I watched her go, and I smiled.

I was her ray of light.

Oh boy.

Day 28

I was her ray of light, but she was everything.

And she needed to be.

The book club was thriving, bursting at the seams. There was never a day when the book she left wasn't taken.

After the test, though, Julie upped her game.

On Day 28, class started as usual, and then Mr Osborne asked a question.

Two hands went up.

Zara, and Julie.

Mr Osborne smiled.

'Well, well, looks like we have some friendly competition here. Fantastic. Okay, Julie, what's your answer?'

Julie answered. She was right. Zara gave a little squeal of delight, turned around and gave Julie a thumbs up.

No one knew what was happening.

Another question.

Two hands.

'Zara? Your turn.'

She was correct, of course.

Julie didn't give a squeal of delight.

Or after the next question, which Zara answered again.

And the next.

Another question.

Two hands.

Even if any of us knew the answers we didn't do anything, we just watched the battle royale as it went on, question after question, and although Julie was smart, although she answered well, she had no chance.

Finally, at the end of class, Zara answered the final question and the class cheered. She had them. They were hers.

Zara stood and raised her arms in mock triumph and, as the bell went, as Mr Gallagher thanked the girls for trying so hard, as Mr Gallagher left, she went over to shake Julie's hand.

Julie sat, stone-faced, arms crossed.

Zara's hand stayed out there, and then she put her hands on the desk, leaned in and whispered, loud enough for those of us close enough to hear.

Loud enough for me to see another side I had wished never existed, but I knew why it did, because of what she had seen, because of what had happened at every other school.

She was being a knight. She was being a ray of light for her, for every other kid who had ever been bullied, she was taking it all on her own shoulders.

For them.

'You don't get to rule anymore,' she said. 'You don't get to push anyone around. We could have been friends. We could have been great friends. But you don't get to ruin nice girls just because it's a game.'

Julie smiled and stood, forcing Zara to take a step back.

'Oh, but I'm going to ruin you. Nice girls? I was *easy* on

them. They didn't do anything to me but be boring and out of place, be with the wrong people. But what you just did, then, that has opened it up. I am going to do more than ruin you. I'm going to destroy you. I want you to leave and never come back.'

I had never been in a room like it.

The silence was a million bees.

Julie looked at me, and her smile changed. She moved past Zara, pushed past her. Zara sighed and picked up her books and went to leave.

In an instant Julie was in front of me, her hand on my chest.

Zara's hand had given me life.

Julie's hand made me recoil.

'You are looking mighty fine today, Hunter,' she said, moving straight back, her hand on me again, testing me straight away, sliding closer to me, using me as the first pawn in her game.

I spun my head, saw Zara at the door, watching, and I saw something in her eyes I never thought I would see.

It was fear.

Fear that she might lose … lose the battle with Julie, lose the fight, lose me, lose everything.

That was all I could see. She had stood up to Julie, and she had won, and now she was going to pay for it, and she was scared.

The storm was coming, but I didn't know this was what it would be.

I didn't know I would be a part of it.

I didn't know if I was ready for this.

But I had to be.

But still I couldn't move, as Julie's hand stroked my chest.

Zara left, her dress swirling behind her, the faintest tinge of blue and grey reaching me as Julie continued to talk, leaning in closer now. She had seen Zara too, seen her face, her eyes, seen her leave, and she knew she was winning.

But she wouldn't win by using me.

I wasn't a pawn.

I wouldn't be taken by anyone.

Almost anyone.

Zara was gone. She wouldn't see what I would do, but that didn't matter. I did it for her anyway, and I did it for me as well.

And I did it for Avril.

I slid Julie's hand off my chest, I sucked down the lump in my throat, and I spoke.

'Not today, Julie. Not any day.'

Julie shoved me in the back as I walked away, making me stumble and making her and her friends laugh.

'Bad move, idiot,' she said. 'Looks like I'm taking down two people now.'

I walked off, heart hammering.

I was in the storm and no, I wasn't ready.

Day 29

On Day 29, she didn't answer questions, didn't raise her hand, didn't give Julie any fuel.

I couldn't believe it.

She was letting Julie win.

It had only taken a day, a moment, but she was letting her win.

Or so I thought.

She didn't even look at me when she came into class. It was like everything that had happened before was gone, like what she thought she'd seen the day before with Julie had ended everything. She walked past me, pastel blues and greys filling my nose, and then she moved on, swirling into her seat, but not moving smoothly, the wind coming in gusts now.

She still wore her scarf, though, and she still wore her usual slightly off-beat clothes, although not as off-beat as usual.

So it wasn't a total back down.

But the others weren't backing off either.

I could see her eyes from where I sat, and I could see they

were grey, clouds gathering, a storm brewing.

Before class began, before there was a teacher in the room, Julie and the others crowded round her, whispering to her, saying things I couldn't hear.

I wanted to hear them.

I needed to.

I wasn't going to let them drive her away like they had Avril.

I edged closer.

'No one likes you,' Julie was hissing. 'Look at you. You try and act all weird, why are you weird? You just want attention. And leaving books for people? That is *so* try-hard. Even Hunter doesn't really like you. You saw how into me he was yesterday. Besides, he always hangs around the pity cases. Always. He even used to speak to Avril Whatshername before she couldn't handle life here anymore.'

Zara slowly turned her head and looked through a gap in the people at me. I stared at her, not moving, wondering what she was thinking, what she was thinking about what was happening and what she was thinking about me.

I remembered going to Avril's house and seeing the For Sale sign up, and then going on, moving past, not strong enough to go and even say goodbye.

Not strong enough to do anything.

We continued to stare at each other. Julie was still talking, but I couldn't hear her words anymore, my world was drowning in grey eyes, sinking, searching and then Julie's hand shot out and grabbed the scarf.

Lightning flashed in Zara's eyes. She was on her feet in an instant, her hand on Julie's wrist, gripping it hard, I could tell, shocking Julie, who still held the scarf.

'No,' Zara said, her voice a whisper that carried across the world. 'Not the scarf.'

Julie's face broke into a grin. She had found it. She had found a weakness, a way in, a way to widen the crack until Zara broke.

They stood there for an eternity.

Finally, Zara broke the silence.

'It seems,' she said, 'that we are at an impasse.'

I almost laughed.

She was amazing.

As she said it, the door began to open. Mr Gallagher. Julie sneered and let go of the scarf, and Zara let go of Julie's wrist.

As she went to her seat, Julie whispered something to Ashleigh I couldn't hear. Her bravado was back, the shock and fear that had registered when her wrist had been grabbed gone, but I still noticed her rubbing her wrist under the table when she sat down.

I still saw the fingerprint marks on her wrist when she let go.

I still saw her shiver slightly as she looked at Zara.

The storm was brewing, and it was close, and Julie wasn't smart enough to run inside and get out of the rain.

I moved my chair back to my desk and looked at Glenn, who raised an eyebrow. I shrugged, truly not knowing what was going on, and having no idea what to do either, but I knew I had to connect with her again.

Without her, I felt like my world had lost its water, like 80% of me was gone.

She had me under her spell.

She owned me.

Day 29 – After School

After school we walked. I hadn't seen her at lunch. I had waited, but she hadn't shown. Then, suddenly, as I walked home after school, she was there, sneaking up behind me, grabbing my hand, squeezing it and spinning me around, her face alight, alive, her eyes everything.

She pulled me close and hugged me, then walked again,

holding my hand, and I went with her, because I had no choice.

It was as though nothing had happened.

I went to talk, but she shushed me.

'Hunter, I know what you did yesterday. With Julie. I'm sorry I left, but I saw her with you, close to you, and all I wanted to do was lash out at her. But I couldn't. I had to be the bigger person, so I had to leave. But all I thought about was you and her, and then, when I knew what you did, when I knew that you didn't …'

Her voice trailed off.

I looked at her, waiting, wanting to know what came next, but she simply winked at me, rocked my world with a smile, and skipped in front of me, talking a mile a minute.

'The book club, Hunter, is amazing, but you already know that. You're there. You're *always* there with me. Of course you are. But people love it, and my books are always gone at lunch. Books sustain me, Hunter. They sustain all of us. They are us on a page.'

Her hand flitted to her scarf every now and then as she spoke, and she moved on now, talking of serious things and talking of crazy things, of how she saw us as animals in a zoo, watched by the giant butterflies on other planets.

'They don't understand so much of what we do,' she said, then, 'Hey! Did you know butterflies taste with their feet? Seriously! Imagine if *we* did that! Would you ever wear shoes again?'

I laughed, enjoying the tension relief it provided, enjoying the fact that she could make me laugh so easily.

'I would,' I said, 'totally would, because what if you were in bare foot and stepped in something nasty?'

'Like what?'

'Oh, I don't know, like dog poo?'

It was a joke, but suddenly the air changed.

She stopped walking, right in front of me, forcing me to stop too. Once again, her hand found my chest, but this time it was to stop me. When she spoke, there was teasing in her voice, but there was hardness too.

'And how do you know that tastes bad? Have you ever tasted it?'

I shook my head, wondering where the sudden turn had come from.

'See, Hunter, this is the problem. We fear so much that we don't know about. We hate things we have never seen or tasted or experienced, things that might be the most amazing and beautiful things of all. We fear things that we can't explain, for the simple reason we can't explain them. Why? Why does explaining something matter so much? We never love something we can't explain, we never love the unknown. We like things because we're told they're good, and we hate and fear things because we're told they're bad. And some things, well …'

Her voice trailed off. She was staring at me, eyes alive, dancing, like there was more to what she was saying than just the words, 93%, but I couldn't see it, couldn't grab it, couldn't get a hold of it. I understood the words though, they made perfect sense, they summed up my life, but the more, the other, the whatever that was underlying what she was telling me, I couldn't get it.

I realised it later, of course, but back then, on Day 29, I couldn't get it, couldn't go deeper.

Or maybe I didn't want to.

So I took her hand off my chest, held it, and started walking again. She didn't come, at first. I had to give a slight pull on her hand, and then she walked with me, but I knew Day 28 was still lingering, despite her energy before.

I knew Day 28 was still there.

The blue sky had gone.

The waves were crashing.

Clouds gathered.

I hunched my shoulders into myself and kept walking.

The chill had found me.

'You know I'm always there for you right, but you know I can't always be there either.'

I looked at Glenn. We had a spare period and were sitting in the common room, just us for the first time in ages.

'It's just, you know,' he said. 'You know what the deal is. You know I would take down Archie if I could, but you know what happened, you know what they said they would do to me.'

I nodded. The "they" wasn't Archie, or the other mean kids at school, it was Glenn's parents and his teachers. Glenn had dreams, dreams of leaving our town, leaving and finding something in the big city, finding the lights and the action. He had said he would do anything, security, cleaning, anything, just to be around the lights and action.

But when he'd defended that kid against Archie, when he'd beaten Archie down, when he'd been the one to cop the trouble, "they" had said they wouldn't let him leave.

"They" wouldn't let him out of there, "they" would find ways to keep him, hold him back, that there would be charges laid unless he accepted full responsibility.

And if he ever did it again …

'It's okay,' I said. 'I know you would if you could.'

'It's just brewing, Hunter. I can feel it, and I know you can too. Things are about to explode. You're going to be in the middle. If you're with her, you're in it too, and I don't know what I can do to help you.'

I nodded again. He was right, I knew he was right, but I wouldn't be anywhere else than by her side, her ray of light.

'She needs me, that's all. And you know I need her too. This is different. This is something else.'

Glenn nodded in return.

'Okay, yeah, I know. Two things though. One, don't forget me, okay? We're a team, you and I, no matter the distance, we're a team. Always have been, always will be. Since Grade 1, right?'

I nodded, and Glenn continued.

'And I've always got your back. I don't know how, but if it comes down to it, I've always got your back. Okay?'

I nodded again, choking up. I had turned my back on Glenn, not in a bad way, but to be with her, and here he was saying he would stand up for me even if it meant losing his dream.

I didn't deserve a friend like him, but I was so glad I had him.

I wouldn't let him down again.

Day 30 – After School

'Do you remember what you asked me on Day 9?'

I spun and stared at her, shocked.

'Day 9?'

'Yes, doofus, Day 9. You know, Day 1 was the first day I came to school, the first day I saw you. Day 9 was the day you spoke to me for the first time. Today is -'

I finished her sentence for her.

'Day 30, after school.'

She nodded.

I felt like we were truly one, that there was no distance between us, no separation, that every thought I had was thought in her head, that every beat of my heart pumped blood through her veins.

My thoughts returned to Day 9, and what I had asked her.

'Why do you wear that scarf every day?' I whispered. 'And why is it black?'

She smiled and nodded, her hand going to the scarf, playing with the end of it, stroking it almost lovingly.

'Hunter, I tell you more than I tell anyone. What I'm about to tell you is for you, and you alone. Promise?'

I promised. She stared into my eyes, my heart, my me, and she nodded.

'This scarf was given to me by my mother. It wasn't

charcoal then, it was blue. And grey. It was meant to protect me from what was happening at school, to give me strength. Like a security blanket.'

I almost laughed, ready to make a joke about a baby and its security blanket, but I caught the words before they got near my mouth.

This wasn't the time for jokes.

'After everything finished, after it was all over and … my mother couldn't handle it all. She couldn't live with what she had allowed to happen, and she …'

Her voice trailed off, but I knew what she had been going to say. I knew how her mother felt, and I had felt the same with Avril, like I had totally let her down, like I should have helped, that because of me she had suffered terribly, and that I wasn't worthy to be here anymore.

I'd had those thoughts.

I had planned things.

I had been lucky.

I'd had Glenn.

He pulled me out of it, saved me.

When it had mattered, he'd been there.

Of course he had.

He had been my best friend, my closest confidante.

Until now.

Because of her.

It was all her.

Her hand rested on my shoulder, and she stared into my eyes, the water calm, peaceful, soothing.

'I'm glad you didn't do it,' she whispered. 'So glad. It isn't something I would wish on anyone.'

I stared back, no longer surprised that she knew what I was thinking, what I was feeling.

She leaned in and kissed me on the mouth, and then, with a sigh, she pulled away, stroking my face, her eyes sad.

'This scarf has become more than I could ever have

imagined. It's more to me than my mother knew. It's more than just a security blanket. It's a symbol of change, of life.'

I didn't move.

I couldn't breathe.

'I know what you were feeling, Hunter, and I know what my mother was feeling, and I know what Avril was feeling, and I know what I was feeling. I was her, and you, and all of you. I am everyone, but I am no one, and I don't understand why, but sometimes, when I meet a boy like you, then I know why I'm here. Then I know my purpose.'

Storm clouds gathered.

She gripped the ends of the scarf.

'Hunter, we are each other, you know that, don't you? We are in each other.'

I nodded, a tiny movement.

I knew.

She stared at me for a long forever, and then the storm was gone, and she flashed a smile, and kissed me quickly.

My hand reached up to her scarf, closing over her hand, holding it. I suddenly found myself longing to see her neck underneath it, longing to see the skin, the smooth skin, to stroke it, feel it, to not miss out on any of her.

They had thought it was a deformity, or a scar, but I knew now it was more than that, that it was nothing to do with her neck, it was deeper than that, and that her neck would be perfect, and even if there *was* a deformity or a scar, it would still be perfect.

They didn't get that. They didn't get that that was too simple, and she was anything but simple.

She was complexity and intricacy.

She was heart and soul.

A scar was an outer image, something on display, and she was the kind of person who would display her scar, not hide it.

'This is me! **LOOK!** Everybody **LOOK!** This is part of me, and part of what makes me beautiful.'

That was what she would do.

So it couldn't be a scar.

But I had no idea what it could be.

I kissed her and pulled on it gently.

She made a small noise and stopped me.

The kiss continued, waves crashing, thunder roaring overhead, loud, trembling lips.

I pulled gently on the scarf.

'I get it,' I whispered into her mouth. 'I don't know all of it, I don't understand all of it, but I get it. Show me. I would do anything for you. I want to see all of you.'

She pressed her forehead against mine, our mouths still together, but not kissing anymore, just there, breathing each other's breath, being with each other.

'Anything?' she breathed.

'Anything.'

She moved my hand away, and then rested hers on my cheek, pulling away so she could look into my soul. She examined me, to see if what I was saying, what I believed, was real, and when she saw it was, she smiled, a half smile, but a smile with life in her eyes.

'Hunter,' she said. 'There's a dance next weekend, you know that, right?'

Of course I did. The posters were everywhere. I had just ignored them, too preoccupied with everything else.

'Well, were you ever going to ask me?'

I shook my head. I hadn't thought she would be into dances.

She threw my hand away in mock disgust, and turned on me.

'Hunter Andrews, I *love* dances! When I dance it's like when I read a book. It's like the real world with all its problems and issues disappears, and I can just be fully, totally me without any judgment or care from anyone. So we'll go? We'll go to the dance?'

I hesitated. I knew school dances. I knew it was where bad

things happened, where boiling points were reached.

She sensed my hesitation and moved in to hold my hands.

'Hunter,' she said, 'the dance will be amazing. Do you trust me?'

I nodded, holding my breath. I did. I trusted her without knowing why or how.

'Good,' she said. 'Good.'

And then she kissed me again, and every thought I had ever had about that scarf disappeared into pastel blues and greys.

Day 32 and 33

We saw Glenn on Saturday morning, and then we spent every moment of the weekend with each other, and with every moment I fell more into her, more under her spell, more in love with her.

I was obsessed.

I was gone, lost, found.

And before I knew it, it was the end of the weekend and she was gone, and I was home, on a Sunday night, and unlike any other student I knew, I couldn't wait for school on Monday.

Day 34, 35, 36, 37, 38

An entire school week.

Five days.

Every one of them was filled with tension, all of us waiting for the next installment of Zara v Julie.

But nothing happened.

Seriously nothing.

Not between them, anyway.

I didn't know that the whispers were just out of our reach, just beyond our hearing, our sight.

I didn't know what was building, because I was in the

bubble.

Zara and I grew closer, and she had joined the group now, Glenn and the others. She still read, and she still left the books out, and we still did book club, but she was with us now, *we* were with us.

And Glenn and the others accepted her, everyone accepted her, how could they not, it was like she had found her place, and she glowed, oh, she glowed and she shone and she sparkled and even though there is no such thing as perfect, she was perfect.

And she kept getting more perfect every day.

Day 39

Saturday night.

The school had organised the dance as a treat, although I didn't doubt they had sensed the tension as well.

They knew, and they wanted something they could control, keep us all under one roof, keep us safe.

They obviously hadn't watched Carrie.

That was all I could think about as I got ready, as I put on my good jeans, and my good t-shirt, and messed up my hair, which counted as doing my hair, all I could think about was Carrie.

That and Zara's voice.

'Do you trust me?'

'The dance is going to be amazing.'

That girl, that perfect, amazing, generous, gentle girl was not capable of harming a fly, but still the thoughts came.

I had seen Carrie.

All I could think about was Julie and her minions dying, all of them, a bloodbath.

But I knew Julie wouldn't go down without a fight.

She never went down without a fight.

She never went anywhere without a fight.

And that meant Zara was in danger too.

I walked to the dance. It wasn't far to get to school, and I needed to walk.

Alone.

All the times I had wanted nothing but her, nothing but us in our bubble, and now, walking to the dance, feeling like this was it, this was the showdown, all I wanted was to be in my own little bubble, my own space and place.

I wanted her but I didn't want her.

I needed her but I didn't want her need her have her I didn't know what I wanted.

It didn't matter.

I know that now, and I should have known that then.

But I didn't.

When I heard the slightest swish of a dress, when I didn't turn around, when suddenly she was there, with me, walking beside me, sliding her fingers through mine, when I was consumed with chills and pastel blues and greys, when her scarf fluttered as she walked and brushed against my neck, tickling it, when I didn't respond, when all of that happened, when I felt in control, I wasn't in control.

It didn't matter what I thought.

She had me under her spell.

When I felt her and touched her and smelt her and all I knew was her.

When she spoke and all I could feel was joy.

When she stopped walking, and looked at me with eyes so blue it looked like they'd been painted on, when she smiled at me, when she rocked my world, when she whispered to me that I owed her a slow dance, that we would dance and no one else there would matter, nothing that had happened or would happen would matter, only *we* would matter, when she did that, and when I looked at her and she nodded, a movement barely even noticeable, when she did that and then turned and started walking again, talking a million miles a minute, pure joy, pure intelligence, pure life, nothing mattered.

No.

Everything about *her* mattered.

Nothing *else* mattered.

I would have gone all Carrie on a hundred Julies right then and there for that moment to continue.

But I knew it wouldn't.

As soon as we walked through the door, I knew it wouldn't.

Because they were there, waiting.

Julie, Archie, Ashleigh, Tracey, Marcus, Sienna, they were all there, together, and as soon as we walked in, they stopped talking, and they stared.

Glenn was off to the side, with our friends, and he watched us come in, and I could tell it took everything he had, every ounce of strength, not because he didn't want to but because he knew now, in front of everyone, even though she had joined us, he had seen them watch us come in as well, and he was officially stating that he was with us, he would defend us, when he waved to us, called us over, that was what he was saying.

Julie spun and fixed her anger onto him, but he shrugged it off, and I loved him then, I loved him like a brother and best friend and saviour, because it actually made it feel like everything was going to be okay.

Only it wasn't.

Just not in the way I expected.

Day 39 – The Dance

A hundred stories have been told about that night.

A hundred tales of what she did, how she looked, what happened at the end.

None of them are true.

Because none of them capture just how wonderful she was that night.

And none of them knew what happened after.

She wasn't at the dance.

She *was* the dance.

As soon as we got there, as soon as Glenn waved us over, she pulled me and she ran and she grabbed Glenn's hand and we went on the dance floor when no one was on the dance floor, and she danced, while Glenn and I stood there, self-conscious, knowing everyone was watching us, knowing everyone was laughing, knowing that we looked stupid and then she grabbed our hands again and she laughed, and that laugh was like a rainbow, where you know it has an end but you never actually want to find it, and she spun us around and eventually we laughed too.

And then no one else existed.

Until they joined us.

First our group, our friends, then a few more, then suddenly it was almost everyone. They danced and they spun and then I wasn't holding her hand anymore, where was she, but I was holding someone else's and it was a circle and then no one was holding hands, we were clapping and dancing and she was in the middle, and she was light and colour and smell and sound.

She caught my eye as she danced, and it was as though everything had been forgotten. All the whispers and the rumours and the threats, it didn't matter.

Julie wasn't there, of course, in the circle, or the others that stuck with her.

They stood off to the side, whispering, plotting, planning, but everyone else danced. It was as though she'd set them free, and some of them, when she rejoined the circle and another person was in the centre, some of them apologised.

'We should have hung out sooner.'

'Can I still join the book club?'

'I read Stargirl with a candle burning.'

She was glowing.

She was alive.

She was life.

She was lifeblood.

She was mine.

A slow dance came on and she walked over to me, swaying her hips, pointing at me, tucking her finger in a come here movement.

'You owe me a slow dance,' she said.

Glenn laughed at me as I stood there, unable to move, transfixed by her, wanting to dance with her but never wanting to not see her walking to me like that.

It was a memory I would have forever.

It's the memory I try and hold above all the others.

Glenn pushed me and I stumbled towards her, regaining my balance and then a second later I was in her arms, and I breathed her in, and I turned my head so my nose and lips were on her neck, above the scarf, below her ear.

She held me close, and she whispered, 'This is perfect.'

And it was

Other couples danced too.

Julie and her people watched, talking every now and then to people when they took a rest from dancing.

I didn't rest from dancing.

I never wanted to stop dancing.

It was the calm before the storm, but the storm never came.

Not that night anyway.

There were a couple of after parties, after the dance, obviously, but I wasn't going to go to them. She said she didn't want to go. I didn't want to go either. As much as I didn't want the night to end, I didn't want the night with her to end.

And besides, my mum didn't like me staying out past midnight.

She was there at the end of the dance, my mum, to pick me up, and Zara came to the car with me.

'Hi, Mrs Andrews,' she said through the car window. 'I'm Zara.'

'Oh,' Mum said, playing it cool, playing it straight. 'The new girl.'

Oh boy.

I hadn't spoken to her about Zara, about anything for a long time, since Avril really, but she had obviously heard about Zara.

In our town, everyone heard about everyone.

Zara laughed, and my heart lost its place.

'That's right, Mrs Andrews. I don't know how long that new girl title lasts, but for now that's me.'

She was charm and she was delight.

'Well, I hope my Hunter treated you well tonight.'

'Oh, he was the perfect gentleman,' Zara said, 'although …'

Her voice trailed off.

Mum raised an eyebrow.

Zara leaned into the window and whispered loud enough for me to hear.

'I have a feeling he wants to kiss me goodnight.'

Oh boy.

My mum, to my complete and utter shock, smiled.

'Well now. Perhaps I should change the radio station, which will obviously require my full concentration.'

What?

Zara spun around, her face alight. How had she done that? I didn't care.

She gave a little squeal and ran at me, her lips finding mine, her hand on the back of my head, her soul entering my body.

She broke off the kiss and stared at me, breathless.

'I need you later,' she whispered. 'I'll come for you.'

Then she kissed me again, quickly, turned to the car and said, 'He's all yours, Mrs Andrews!' then she ran off, leaving both of us watching her, both of us wondering if she was real, for entirely different reasons.

Day 39 – After the Dance

I lay in bed, in just my jeans, my mind whirling with the night, whirling like she had whirled, like she had whirled Glenn and I.

Everything was whirling, and everything that had happened before, any thoughts I'd had about her getting revenge on Julie, any thoughts Julie had about getting her, the test, the questions, none of it seemed real.

It all seemed like a dream that I had woken from, and while I was fuzzy and woolly, I also was as clear as I had ever been.

She was the most amazing person I had ever met.

Would ever meet.

And then.

On the window.

A tap.

Like a little rock being thrown.

Tap.

Another one.

I got out of bed and walked to the window, starting back as I saw a shadow disappear.

It was just the trees.

Just a shadow.

I opened the window, and there she was, looking up at me, tossing rocks to and fro in her hand.

'Hey there, sleepy head,' she said, her voice a whisper, reaching me with ease. 'Nice chest.'

I blushed.

'Hey there,' I said, running my hand through my hair, trying to casually flex my bicep without seeming to flex my bicep, wondering what.

That was all.

Wondering what.

Any word could have come after that and it would have worked.

I was wondering what.

I soon found out.

'Well, come on then. Haven't you heard? There are things to do. There are adventures to be had.'

I hadn't heard.

No one had told me.

Her face was lit up, her smile a lighthouse I could have seen from miles away.

Without a word I threw on a top and ran downstairs.

I knew Mum wouldn't be rapt with me going out now, so late, but I also knew that she had liked Zara, had let me kiss Zara, basically right in front of her, so I figured it would be okay.

I figured my midnight curfew could be stretched out a little.

I figured I was going anyway.

I ran out the door and I ran to her, and when I reached her I grabbed her and I held her so close it was like our bones merged.

'You've saved me,' I said.

I felt her smile.

'And now it's your turn to save me,' she whispered.

I went cold.

I froze.

Save her from what?

I broke off the hug and she looked straight into my eyes, like she did, and then she kissed me, so deeply and passionately and tenderly that when it ended, my neck craned forward a little, searching for more, longing for more.

She took my hand and we ran into the night.

It was ours, this night, ours alone.

We could do anything.

And we did.

I had wondered, never out loud, never consciously even, where she lived.

What her mum was like.

Now.

It hadn't mattered.

We always found each other.

Always been together.

Where she lived didn't matter, but now she took me there.

We ran there.

It was an old house, single story, neat, tidy, one I didn't remember, which was weird, because I had ridden these streets as a kid, over and over again.

Even the street was one I didn't remember, but then there were new estates that had gone up since I was little, and it was dark, and I was with her, and we could have run anywhere and I would have gone and not known where we were because I was with her, that was where I was, *she* was where I was, everything else was scenery.

We ran up and she opened the door.

It was unlocked, which was also weird, as no one left their door unlocked, not these days.

Everyone was scared, nervous, worried about being broken into.

I liked that she didn't worry about that.

That she trusted people.

It felt nice.

Old school.

As she went in, I held her back.

She spun around, her face a beautiful mixture of concern and excitement.

She raised an eyebrow at me.

'Your mum?' I asked. 'Is it okay for me to be here?'

She laughed, quietly, but loud enough to send butterflies raging through my stomach.

Then she moved in close and kissed me, speaking to me as our lips touched.

'Hunter, my mum's away tonight, but even if she were here, all she wants is for me to be happy. That's all she ever wanted. It killed her that she couldn't at those other schools, that I was so upset at what happened to those girls, and that's why we keep moving, that's why it's a new school every year, she just wants to find somewhere perfect for me to fit into. And now she has. Because now I have you and there was the dance and there's everything. It's perfect. I love it. Hunter?'

My heart stopped.

Time stopped.

Was she really going to say it?

I knew it. I felt it. I lived it. But I hadn't said it, not to her, not to anyone.

She said it.

'I love you, Hunter Andrews. I love you one hell of a lot.'

And then she turned and ran, letting go of my hand, making me chase her through the house, past the lounge, carpeted, the kitchen, tiled, and down the corridor, carpeted.

We reached her room and she stopped, her hand on the handle, and again her voice changed.

'So, Hunter, this is it. The room of the weird girl. Do you dare to enter?'

I laughed.

I dared.

I double dared.

'I dare,' I said, changing my voice as well, making it as deep as I could. 'Nothing scares the mighty warrior.'

She laughed like it was the funniest thing she had ever heard, and I couldn't help but join in.

When she finally recovered, she took an overly dramatic deep breath, opened the door, stepped to the side and waved her hand.

'Well, then. Come on in. Enter the cave of doom.'

I entered.

It was amazing.

It was her.

It sparkled.

Literally.

Fairy lights hung from the roof and the walls. Her bed was perfect, her desk holding notebooks and gemstones and it was her, the whole room was her and it was perfect.

She was perfect.

She sat on the bed and watched me.

'You can touch things, you know,' she said. 'If you want.'

I walked over to her and stroked her hair behind her ear.

'I want,' I said.

Who *was* I?

She laughed and pulled me onto the bed with her, and we kissed, and then it was more than kissing, it was everything, it was a joining, it was my first time and it was perfect. She held me and guided me and was me, she knew me.

And I was her.

We were one in our bubble and everything, everything was perfect.

Everything was perfect.

Day 40

The day after the dance.

I had run home, early, from her place, to be in bed before Mum realised I'd even been out.

I ran on air.

No.

Too cliché.

I floated on air.

Wait.

That's worse.

I got home, and although I didn't make a sound, everything was singing.

Everything.

I went to bed and I fell asleep and then I woke up, and all I wanted to do was see her, be with her.

I called her, but she didn't answer.

I messaged.

Nothing.

I started to feel tense, worried.

Had I not been good?

Had I done something wrong?

Had her mum come home, and had she known what we had done in her house?

Had something something something why wasn't she replying?

I got up and dressed.

Mum was downstairs, eating breakfast.

She smiled at me, and I smiled back, heck, I was already smiling when I walked in the room, the nervous smile of I want to be found out I don't want to be found out.

'Hunter, I want to thank you for coming home after the dance last night. I know there were after parties, and I know I like you to be home, which is hard for you. I know last night was a big thing for you. So it means a lot that you came home.'

I kept smiling and I nodded, scared to speak and give everything away, and then I went and got some cereal.

I thought about her saying she didn't want to go to the party.

Had she really wanted to go?

Had she lied to me?

She had lied with me, I knew that.

I laughed out loud, the crude joke breaking the tension.

'Hunter?'

Oh.

Mum was still there.

Of course.

I poured my cereal and turned to sit next to her.

'It's nothing, Mum. Just remembering the dance.'

Mum smiled, and it was a smile that showed she knew everything.

'Yes, I heard it was quite the dance. I heard you and that Zara girl -'

'Danced!'

The word blurted out before I could stop it, before she could say anything else.

I had said it too loud and too sharp and too fast, obviously covering up, but Mum just smiled.

'Yes, Hunter, you danced. I know. All night. And I'm not stupid. The radio didn't need adjusting, you know.'

I knew.

But she didn't know.

Not everything.

It was a relief though, that she didn't, because everything was too much.

It was feeling like too much for me.

A knock on the door startled me, and my spoon jerked in the cereal.

'Hunter, what's going on? You seem about to jump out of your skin.'

'Huuuuuuuuuuuuuunterrrrrrrrrrrrr.'

Her voice sang from the front door, and I felt myself blush. Mum laughed out loud now, then walked over and hugged me.

'Oh Hunter, you are **SO** cute! My little boy's in love.'

I was, but she didn't realise how deeply.

She went to the door and opened it.

'Hello, Zara.'

'Helloooooo, Mrs Andrews. Can Hunter come out and play?'

I heard Mum laugh again, and I liked it. Zara did that. She brought out the best in people.

She raised their energy.

I finished my cereal and dropped the bowl in the sink, then walked to the door, resisting the almost overpowering urge to run.

'Hey,' I said, playing it cool.

'Hey,' she said, imitating my voice, mocking me in a way that made me want her more, dammit.

Mum laughed again and pushed me out the door.

'Have fun, you two. Home before dark, remember. School night.'

I nodded and walked out.

Zara turned and smiled at mum with a half rock my world smile.

'Don't worry, Mrs Andrews. He'll be home like a good boy.'

Then she pushed me so I ran down the stairs, and she was right behind me, and we ran off, holding hands and laughing, and she'd said I would be home before dark, and I was.

Day 41

On Day 41, at school, Julie made her move. She had obviously started setting things up at the dance, with the whispers when people rested, and also on the Sunday, after the dance, and on Monday it started.

It started with Julie herself, of course, walking up to us as we sat at lunch, on the table now, with Glenn and the others.

Julie, with Archie behind her, Ashleigh, Tracey, Marcus, Sienna, the whole gang.

Just them this time.

Behind them, everyone else watched.

Waiting to see how it went.

To see who had the strength, who held the upper hand.

To see who won.

To see which side they would choose.

Our table stopped too, except for Zara.

Always except for Zara.

She was telling a story, and she wouldn't stop, and I wanted her to but didn't want her to.

But I had to.

I put a hand on her arm, resting it there. She turned and smiled at me, still talking and then she raised her eyes and smiled at Julie as well.

But she didn't stop, didn't take my hint.

The story continued.

'Shut up!' Julie eventually screamed. 'For the love of God, please shut up!'

Julie was losing it, but she had cards up her sleeve, cards she knew would hit home.

Zara stopped talking then, and the smile lessened, but it was still there, crooked, curious, baiting.

It was the first time I'd noticed it.

It had always felt like Julie was the one baiting, charging, stirring.

But Zara was doing it now, too.

Or had she always been doing it?

Did part of her want this?

Had this been her plan all along *NO!* Why was I suspicious of her? Was I scared I was falling too fast, falling too deep, for someone that was about to be taken down the same way Avril had been taken down? Did I want Zara to want the fight, to stand up, to beat Julie, because then I wouldn't have to do it for her? I wouldn't have to be the ray of light I *wanted* to be the ray of light!

I didn't want Zara to be tarnished.

I wanted her to stay perfect.

But there is no such thing as perfect.

Perfect is an illusion.

Julie put both her hands on the table, leaning forward.

Under her left hand was a book.

When she spoke, her voice was back in control.

'You think you have what it takes?'

No response.

The smile stayed.

Julie's face went red.

She wanted something, anything, something she could lash out at without having to go first. She didn't want to strike the first blow, not outwardly, but she wanted this to begin before she looked silly.

'You think you're so much better than us,' she said,' 'but you're not, you know. You have your old clothes, and you have the boy and you have the dance. And you have your books, the books you read, the books you give away, the books you talk about.'

Zara spoke for the first time.

'Oh, I don't give them away,' she said, her voice light, seemingly confused. 'I just leave them. You have to understand, Julie. We don't find books. Books find us. They connect with us and they live within us. The same book can unearth a different story for every person. I left the books. People took the books. It was perfect.'

You are perfect.

Julie sneered.

'You talk, and you use words, but it's all an act. I know it's all an act. You're an emo without being an emo, pretending to be something just for effect.'

Now Zara did look hurt.

She was the most genuine person I had ever known, and she defined herself by it, by honestly expressing herself.

By being her.

And now she was hurt someone was accusing her of being untrue to herself.

Or at least, that's why I thought she was hurt.

Julie smiled.

She had her.

Or at least, she thought she had her.

'Julie, how can you say that? Emos aren't fake. They have a way they believe is their true self, and for them it is true, so you can't say that. It's disrespectful. It's a gift we can give them, to believe that they are following a path that brings them happiness through sadness.'

Julie fumed. She had thought she had Zara on the run, and then it was flipped back at her. This was like watching an artist create a masterpiece.

I was in awe.

Everyone was.

Zara had her.

She had the strength and she had the upper hand and she would have the people on her side.

But then Julie played her trump card of the day.

'Well, we have a gift for you, faker. We have books for *you*, books that tell your story. And trust me, they tell a story that we *all* believe is true.'

She lifted her hand, and she turned over the book she'd been leaning on.

It looked like a normal book, but it wasn't.

There was a picture of Zara on the cover, looking amazing, but that wasn't the point.

Julie read out the title, loud enough for everyone to hear.

Look at my stupid clothes I bought a hundred years ago.

Julie laughed and stepped back. Archie stepped forward and lay a book next to the first one.

Zara was on the cover again, the same picture.

Archie read out the title.

I can't take this scarf off because my neck is deformed.

Ashleigh next.

Another book.

Another title.

I dance like an idiot to cover up that I can't dance.

Tracey.

I think I'm better than everyone.

Marcus.

I am soooooooo smart.

Sienna.

Nobody likes me, and nobody ever will.

They read them again, all of them, again and again and over and over. Zara stared at the books as they laughed and as they read, each title repeated over and over like water dripping into my brain until I stood up and I shouted, '***ENOUGH!***'

I shouted, '***STOP!***'

'Hunter, no!' Zara screamed.

They stopped.

They stopped reading out the titles and laughing and pointing and they turned their focus to me.

'Finally,' Julie said. 'Archie?'

Archie stepped forward. I didn't flinch, even though every single fibre I had begged me to, even though my heart felt like it was about to push my eyes out of my head.

I stayed there, because I was her ray of light.

Archie got closer, but before he reached me, a shadow moved between us.

Glenn.

Always Glenn.

'Do you really want to go there, Archie,' he said, his voice low, almost a growl.

Archie hesitated.

'Well *you* can't, Archie replied, 'or it's over for you, Sunshine.'

'Get him, Archie. Get both of them!' Julie ordered.

Archie hesitated. He wanted to, he certainly wanted to get me, but he knew what Glenn was capable of.

He had felt what Glenn was capable of.

He knew what Glenn could do if he ignored the consequences of beating the hell out of Archie.

Again.

So Archie stared, and then he leaned past Glenn and he pointed at me.

'Your turn's coming,' he said, and I knew he was right.

My turn was coming.

Archie turned and hooked Julie's arm though his.

'Not today, babe,' he said as they walked off, minions in tow. 'Let's make him sweat. Let's make him wonder when it's coming.'

'Well, he'll never sweat any other way,' Ashleigh said, and they all laughed.

I noticed other people laughing too, people who had danced with us only a few days before, now they were weighing up their options.

They knew they had crossed Julie by dancing with us, she would have told them that, she wasn't a subtle dictator, and so they knew what the safer option from here would be.

And it wasn't with us.

The balance had swayed with the books, and with me standing up.

We watched them go, then I sat down, Glenn too.

Zara smiled at us both.

'My two brave knights,' she said. 'My two brave, gallant knights.'

And then she went back to telling her story, but there had been a shift.

I could feel it in the air.

The storm was brewing, and when it hit, I wanted to be her shelter.

Even if it killed me.

Day 42

Day 42.

The worst day of my life.

I had been in love before, or at least thought I had.

With Avril Matthews.

And that hadn't ended well.

It sounds stupid now, that I was in love back then, of course it does, I was 13, but it made me hold back now, how I had let it end. I dug myself into a hole and then every time I held back I dug that hole a little deeper, until it was all the way to the centre of the earth and I couldn't stop digging, even though I knew I needed to, I had to.

It sounds stupid now.

It wasn't stupid.

I had been in love.

But it hadn't been enough.

I hadn't been able to let love outweigh my fear of social rejection.

I hadn't let it allow me to be brave.

Vulnerable.

I didn't know if I would be able to do it now, for her, no matter how much I thought I wanted to, when the moment came, would I turn away, a face in the crowd?

There are moments in life where we let ourselves be vulnerable, let ourselves show the world who we really are, and nine times out of ten, when we do this, we will be shot down, it will come back to bite us. It can be truly devastating, but that is exactly why we have to do it, exactly why we have to get shot down, hurt, because that's when we find strength, that's when we realise that yes, if we get back up, if we go again, everything is going to be okay.

That was my problem.

I hadn't realised that.

Not with Avril.

I hadn't realised it can happen over and over and we have to keep getting back up.

I thought I had one chance.

I thought I had failed, and I had, but I thought that meant I had failed forever.

But forever is a long time, and back in 8th grade, and 9th grade and 10th and 11th, all those years I held myself back, didn't open up, through my parents taking me to therapists, trying to find out why I was so closed off, why I wouldn't talk to them about things, talk to them at all really, why I didn't write anymore, through all that, in the end all it took was Zara.

All anything took was her, whatever that means.

With a twirl of her dress, with books left on a seat, with a laugh that set me free, she let me be alive again.

She was everything I ever wanted.

That was why Day 42 was the worst day of my life.

Not that she did anything wrong, not at first.

Not that she did anything wrong at all.

In fact, even after what had happened the day before, she was still laughing, still strong, still beautiful.

No, it wasn't because of that, that's not why, I'm not saying it right, I don't know how to … it was because of *her*, who she was, how she was, it was because of her laugh, her energy.

It was because they were trying to destroy something so amazing.

They had gone after her with the fake books, and she had picked up every one of them and taken them home with her.

She had stood tall.

On Day 42 they tried again, little things in class, notes, whispers, giggles, pokes, prods.

The group doing it was larger.

Growing.

Through it all I was by her side, I stayed with her, I wouldn't let her go through this alone, I was there.

Then it was lunch.

Day 41 had taken a chink out of Zara's armour, I knew it had, but it hadn't been enough.

Not for Julie.

I thought she'd played her trump card, but I was wrong.

All she'd done was lead, let us think it as all she had, but the Joker was still in her hand.

On Day 42, at lunch, as we sat at the table, some of us playing cards, Zara reading a book, all of us content, they appeared again, only this time it wasn't just Julie and her gang.

It was everyone.

It wasn't everyone.

It felt like everyone.

Everyone we had thought was on our side, everyone we knew wasn't, they were all there.

And they all held a book.

This time it wasn't fake ones.

These were the ones she had left beside her, the ones people had picked up, so eager to read them, or so I had thought, but that hadn't been the reason, or even if it had been it wasn't now, no, now they were a weapon, a devastating weapon they could use against her, and as they stood in front of us, on Day 42, as she sat, book in hand, looking up at them, her eyes wide, the darkest blue, not a blue of light and energy as it usually was, but a blue of sadness and pain, as book by book, one by one, first Julie, then everyone, they stood in front of her and they tore them apart, ripping pages out of them, and with every page I saw her wince, I saw her feel it as though she were the book itself, that they were tearing up a part of her, taking it out of her and throwing it on the ground.

I stood up again, to stop them, no fear, I was her ray of light, but this time they grabbed me, Glenn too when he tried to help, but there were too many of them this time, not just Archie.

They held him back, and they held me back, held me down, hands gripping me so hard it hurt inside the muscle and bone, Archie punching me now, hard in the stomach, shoving me against the ground and then lifting me up, laughing at my feeble struggle, at my cries, making me watch her, telling me that this was my fault too, after yesterday, and that they would come for me when she was done, that they would finish her, ruin her, and that they would make me watch and then, after I had seen them take down someone stronger than me, after I would already be broken from watching that, they would finish me off.

They were like wild animals.

Where were the teachers?

Where was anyone, someone, *anyone?*

They told me all that as they made me watch, and now she wasn't looking at the books anymore, wasn't looking at the pages float to the ground, she was staring straight at me, and I saw her eyes change, I saw them change from blue sadness to grey and back again, and then the darkest grey, a storm that will destroy, Julie sneering, 'I hope this hurts you everywhere, and that the pain never stops,' Ashleigh screeching, 'Look at her, she's gutted!',

Marcus screaming, 'Oh her poor eyes, she wishes she couldn't watch,' Tracey screaming, 'Tear them apart!', Sienna screaming, 'Look at Hunter's little heart breaking,' Archie holding me, hard, laughing whispering in my ear, 'I hope this hurts you real bad, right in your soul,' and suddenly I couldn't even hear them anymore, I couldn't hear the laughter and the taunting and the cheers and the whispers as every page was torn from every book, as the mob fell in with the bullies, praying that would keep them safe from the same fate, but I couldn't hear anything, we were in our bubble and there was nothing, no one but us, and those eyes, they were flashing, from blue to grey, thunder rolling in, the storm was coming, and then they moved between us, realising that we were holding each other up, that we were enough, that they couldn't get to us like this, and they moved between us, Julie moved between us, and they shoved me next to Zara, and Julie stood there and she held Stargirl, the book I had read with a candle burning, the book that changed me, us, everything, and she tore it to pieces, slowly, making us both watch, and then, as the last page fell to the ground they let us go, and now the teachers were there, asking what the mess was, and I fell to the ground, to my knees, picking up the pages of the book that had been the ignition, the spark that had first joined us, and I tried to put it back together but I couldn't, and now I could hear the laughter, I could hear it fading as they walked away from us, and why wasn't she helping me, why wasn't she on the ground with me, trying to put the pieces back together, why wasn't she there, and then I turned and looked and I saw her eyes, and I saw they weren't sadness blue anymore, they weren't the grey of death, they were a blue of the clearest lagoon, and she was crying, her eyes pools of water that should have been bringing pleasure but that were ripped apart like the books I held in my hands, and through the tears she was asking why was it happening again, why was it exactly the same, every time it was the same, what was *wrong* with people, what was wrong with *her*, why were they coming after *her* and I realised now, as this crack opened her up, that it hadn't been a friend at the last school, or the one before that, or the one before that, it had been *her*, that *she* had been the one who hadn't been able to take it anymore, that *she* was the one who had left and that life had just gone on, Tuesday, Wednesday, Thursday, and she was sobbing now, and so was I, but I was on my feet, grabbing her shoulders and making her stand, teachers asking what was going on, and we left, we walked out, and I didn't care about the laughter or the stares or the teachers' shouts, I didn't care about what would happen to us if we didn't come back that day, I didn't care, I just needed to get her out of there and I needed to get her somewhere safe where she could talk to me tell me be held by me, I wanted to put all of me into her, the best of me, the least of her, joining together to make her whole again, to glue the pages of her book back together, to tell her that there would be Tuesdays and Wednesdays and Thursdays but that they would only matter if she was there, that life wouldn't just go on if she left, that it wouldn't have back then either, that maybe she thought it did but how could a world go on without her in it, how could it possibly, how could *my* world go on without her in it, and then she stopped walking and I turned to her, and I looked at her, and her eyes had changed again, and my heart stopped, because they weren't thunderstorm grey, they weren't storm is coming grey, they were steel grey, they were metal grey, they were a grey that had had life and feeling sucked out of it, and fear tore through me as it looked like I had lost her, that we had all lost her, that she was gone, and then she held me, close, and she whispered in my ear, and she told me that everything was going to be okay, that she knew it was, that this time was different, that she had me, that I was her light, her ray of light, and that she loved me, she loved me so much, and that it gave her strength and comfort and that I always had to live from my heart, that I had so much I held back, and that it was time to let go, to not hold back, that she wasn't going to hold back anymore, and that she wanted me, all of me, she wanted me to give her the best of me, and I nodded because I couldn't speak, all I could see in my mind were those eyes, and then she broke off the hug and looked at me, and her eyes were back to blue, all traces of grey, death, fear, steel, gone and she was with me again, and I was drowning in her and I made myself forget how to swim because to swim would be to escape and all I wanted, right then, was to drown with her, in her, to be by her side no matter what, and then, when she kissed me, when she joined us, it was like she took everything out of me and made it more, made it more her, and she put it back into me and I felt like I wasn't drowning anymore I was flying, and I was so high I was petrified and I knew that with every second I was both finding and losing myself, and I didn't care, that I was her and she was me, and that together everything was going to be okay, and that I never wanted the kiss to end.

And for a long time it didn't.

And, with what came after, I wish it hadn't, because that kiss was the last comfort I would feel for a long time.

Day 43

Do you know that moment? The one when you realise a storm is on its way? Well, I'd known one was coming for a while, but I thought it would pass, but now, on Day 43, it was that moment.

The one where you step outside, and you can smell it.

You can smell the storm in the air.

It's a particular smell, and in Summer, when the ground is hot, and you're barefoot, and you smell it, and you look up, and the sky is black, not right above you black, but close, and the air is as still as it could ever be, and then there is a drop, a single drop, and you know it's coming, and you have a choice.

Run inside and be safe and dry

Or dance in the rain.

On Day 43, I stepped outside, I smelt the storm, and I saw the first drop splatter on the pavement.

And I danced in the rain.

Day 44

I found a poem, one I had written for Avril, back when I wrote, but had been too weak to give her.

I had wanted to.

I had wanted to so much, but in the end my heart wasn't strong enough, which, with what was to come, was interesting.

It had been the last thing I had written.

After the books though, after Day 42, I found it, and when I stepped into the storm, I did it by rewriting the poem, by adjusting it, by making it more her, and then I gave it to Zara.

On Day 44, I sucked it up, I told myself that I had to do this, and I did it.

I gave her *Hell No*.

HELL NO!

Will life always be easy?
Hell no.
Will things always go as planned?
Hell no.
Will people act the way you want, say the things you want, do the things you want?
Hell no.
Will you avoid pain?
Hell no.
When it feels like too much.
When it all feels too hard.
When you're tired.
Overwhelmed.
Worn out.
Worn down.
Will you give up?
Will you quit?
Will you run away and hide?

Will you stop giving because no-one else gives?
Hell no.
Say it.
HELL
NO!
Say it to everyone who has ever held you back.
HELL NO!
Say it to everyone who has ever put you down.
HELL NO!
To everyone who shut you up, drowned you out, brought you back to earth.
HELL NO!
*You will **not** be dragged down.*
*Your will will **not** be weakened.*
When life closes in around you, choking you, crushing you, making it hard to breathe, you will not fall.
You will rise above.
You will not be defeated, because you are strong.
You will not stop living, because you are strong.
*You will take risks, you will live life, you will fall and you will get up and you will show the world that **you … are … strong**.*
You
Are
Strong.
So forget hell no.
Forget proving anything to anyone else.
Forget the haters, because they get their strength from making others feel weak.
Don't say hell no to them.
Say hell yes to life.
And then see what happens.

I gave it to her, and I told her to read it when she was alone, with a candle burning.

She smiled, and hugged me, and later that night, when I

was in bed, wondering if she'd read it, a message came through.

I read it, smiled, and turned over to go to sleep.

She had read it, and she had liked it.

Her message had said one thing.

I knew you were the one. Tomorrow, we say hell yes.

Day 45

Fridays were dull days at school. Dull subjects, dull teachers, dull assemblies, dull dull dull.

But not this Friday.

Not on Day 45.

Because Sienna was sick.

While this may not seem strange, out of the ordinary, and with anyone else it wouldn't be, but with Sienna, this was groundbreaking.

See, Sienna Rowe had never been sick.

Ever.

She'd never been sick and she'd never missed a day of school.

Not a day of kindergarten, not a day of primary school, not a day of high school.

She'd played every game of netball, been in every performance, at every dance, she'd been at everything.

Never had a sniffle, a cough, a tummy ache, nothing.

It was her thing.

Her parents said that even when she was a kid, she hadn't ever thrown up.

She was a machine.

She also longed to be Julie's main offsider, a role that went to Ashleigh, alongside the boyfriend, Archie.

Sienna Rowe was on the next level.

The second level.

The friend, but not the best friend.

Always slightly on the outer.

It was the only way she wasn't number one.

But on Day 45, usually the dullest day of the week, Sienna Rowe was sick.

When she turned up to school, she looked paler than usual. Not much, but enough.

Everyone noticed it, but no one said anything.

Not to her at least.

But the whispers started up.

Sienna sat down in her usual seat, one desk across from Julie, who looked her up and down.

And Julie said something.

Always Julie.

'What the hell, Sienna?' Julie asked. 'What the actual hell?'

Sienna shrugged and coughed, catching her breath as she did so, obviously feeling the cough deeper inside her than anyone else would.

It was like all the illnesses she had avoided her entire life had come back to get her.

Zara swished into the room, blues and greys, eyes alight, seeing me and lighting up my day with a smile, with paper in her hand, a poem in her hand, then seeing Sienna and looking worried.

She swished past me, barely brushing me but brushing me enough, and then she was at Sienna's desk, hand on her back, 'Sienna, what is it? Are you okay?', and then hugging her from behind, and I saw her lips move, whispering something to Sienna, who nodded.

Julie was on her feet in an instant.

'Get away from her, *freak*,' she spat. 'Get away from her.'

Ashleigh stood too, and Archie, and me.

Glenn watched, calm but ready.

Zara looked at us all, wide-eyed, innocent, naive, beautiful.

'But Julie, look at her. She's a sick girl. I think she needs to go home.'

Julie moved over and pushed Zara out of the way, glaring

at her and then putting her arm around Sienna, obviously wishing she had been the first one to do it, but she had been too shocked.

'Sienna Rowe doesn't get sick. Everyone knows that.'

Zara didn't know.

She didn't know Sienna never got sick. How could she?

I looked at Sienna, who was staring up at Zara now, and suddenly she looked worse than ever, the change so quick.

Everyone else was looking at Zara, waiting, but Sienna's eyes were pleading.

'Help me. Please help me. Make it stop. It feels like …'

Her voice trailed off into nothing, the void. Julie spat death with her eyes. Archie moved in as well, holding Sienna, helping her up.

'Come on, Sienna, you have to go. You have to go to sick bay.'

'I don't get sick.'

Her voice was barely a whisper, and pain rode every word.

Archie helped her up, but Sienna didn't even seem to notice. She had aged twenty years in a minute, her skin grey, her hand on her chest. She kept staring at Zara.

'Please, Zara, please make it stop. My heart. It's breaking. I can feel it breaking.'

Zara went over and Julie pushed her away again, making her stumble against chairs, tables, people. I was over in an instant, helping her balance

'Get off,' Julie screamed. 'She's mine, my best friend and you can't steal her off me. She. Is. Mine!'

Ashleigh went to speak then changed her mind, said nothing.

This wasn't the time for technicalities.

'No!' Sienna screamed as they took her away, seemingly using all her energy to speak, barely able to lift her arm above her shoulder as she pointed at Zara. 'Her! It has to be her! Only she can -'

And then she fainted, and Archie wasn't ready for it.

Sienna crashed to the ground through his arms, her head hitting the floor, the noise bursting through all of us, Zara flinching the most, as though the sound itself actually struck her.

But she didn't move forward.

Not this time.

Miss Little came into the room as the bell went, ready to teach, and she was confronted with a crowd of kids around Sienna, unconscious on the floor. She sprang into action, and in an instant Sienna was being carried to sick bay by Archie and Marcus, Julie, Ashleigh and Tracey by her side.

As it all happened, I watched Zara. Only her. She absorbed the whole thing, her face so concerned it was as though she was feeling Sienna's pain now, and maybe she was. Maybe it was like when she read a book, maybe she took it all on.

As soon as Sienna was out of the room though, the switch flicked and Zara sat in her chair, ready for the lesson, while the rest of us milled around, unsure of what to do. Ms Little told us all to sit, and so we did, and she assured us we would be kept updated.

Julie, Archie, Ashleigh, Tracey and Marcus didn't come back to class. They had gone to the sick bay with Sienna, and we heard soon after they went to hospital with her as well.

But it didn't matter.

Them being there couldn't help her.

At 3:25pm, five minutes before school finished for the day, in her private hospital room, Sienna Rowe's heart was that of a 95 year old, and not a healthy one. At 3:25pm, everything stopped.

Sienna Rowe, who had never been sick a day in her life, was dead.

Day 46

The entire town was in a daze.

People didn't die in the town we lived in … well, that obviously wasn't true, but not kids.

And certainly not like that.

Not like … I couldn't even explain it.

She had aged in front of our eyes, like even though she was still a kid, like us, she had withered up and dried out, like all the life had been sucked out of her.

Like her heart had literally broken.

That was what she had said.

I remembered it so clearly now.

'My heart. It's breaking. I can feel it breaking.'

Just like mine had been when they were … she had said it then too.

No.

Not said it.

Screamed it.

With glee.

'Look at Hunter's little heart breaking.'

She had danced around, tearing out pages, people cheering in the background, and she had screamed that.

I wanted to stop it, but I couldn't help feeling a feeling of irony, of satisfaction, and I tried to close it down but I couldn't, I couldn't, it just rose in me and was about to burst out, and I left my room, and I went downstairs to tell Mum, to tell her about the connection, to tell her maybe it was my fault somehow.

'Mum?'

I went into the kitchen, and she was there, on the phone.

As soon as I walked in, she said she had to go, and she hung up.

'It's okay, you can keep talking,' I said.

She shook her head.

'Not now. I'll call back later. It was just …'

She paused, looking at me, as if weighing up whether or not to tell me something.

My stomach churned, a tiny bit.

'Who were you speaking to?' I asked, although I already knew.

'It was the psych. I think perhaps you should go and speak to her again, after, well, after what happened to poor Sienna Rowe.'

I sighed and sat down. I had hated going to the psych, had refused to talk, mostly, and when I had I'd given away so little they hadn't really been able to do anything to help.

Which was fine by me, while it wasn't.

I wanted help, to deal with what I was feeling about Avril, to talk about why I had planned to do certain things, to myself, but I hadn't wanted to talk.

But I did now.

Just not in the way Mum thought.

I wanted to at least tell Mum about the ridiculous connection between Sienna and me.

I looked at her, and I went to speak, and as I did, as I sucked in that tiny bit of air, there was a knock on the door, so I never said a word.

I almost jumped out of my skin though, I'd been so in the moment. Mum jumped too, and then she went to the door.

'Hi, Mrs Andrews.'

It was her.

It was Zara.

Come to see me.

Come to save me.

I got up and walked to the door. My mum was hugging her, holding her close, and Zara was holding my mum, her eyes closed, her face as relaxed as I had ever seen it, contented, soaking up all the hug my mum had to give.

She'd needed that hug.

I wondered if her mum ever hugged her.

I wanted to hug her.

She opened her eyes and saw me, and she smiled, not a rock your world smile, but a touch your heart smile.

'Can Hunter come out and play?' she asked my mum, repeating the words of Day 40, but saying them in a voice that had no joy in it.

And she still hadn't let go of the hug.

'Of course, sweetie,' Mum said, giving her one last squeeze and then pulling back, holding Zara's shoulders, looking at her. 'You two need each other in times like this, to hold each other up, to help each other be strong.'

'Hell yes we do, Mrs Andrews,' Zara said, and my heart held her.

Mum didn't get the reference, but she nodded and then turned to me, and her eyes were moist, and she hugged me.

'Hunter, if you need to talk to Zara first, you do that, but I'm always here for you, okay? Always. What happened with Sienna, it was … it was so sad, but she's gone now, and you're still here, and I love you. Okay?'

I nodded into the hug. It was a hug like she'd given me after Avril had moved away, a hug full of mother. I hugged her back and then, holding Zara's hand, I stepped out the door and into the storm.

Her hand stroked her scarf over and over as we walked. We had held hands to start with, but now we walked separately.

She stroked her scarf, in her own world, her own thoughts, and I was lost in the coming storm.

The smell was stronger now, drops falling at large intervals, but they were large drops.

Even without us speaking I could feel it in the air, Sienna hung over us like a cloud, ready to burst.

For hours we walked, and not a word was said between us, although a million words were in my head and, I'm sure, in hers as well.

Or were there?

How did she think?

Was it in words? That seemed too simple.

She would think in images and colours and sounds and smells, she would think in full technicolour movie blast your mind thoughts.

I thought in words.

I couldn't see things, couldn't visualise, but I knew she would be able to.

I knew she would be able to do anything.

Anything.

I thought of her past schools, and what had happened to her, and I wondered why. Why couldn't people see her? Why couldn't people accept her? What was it about her that made her the target, although even as I thought it I knew the answer, but the stupid thing was the things that made her a target were the things I loved about her most.

She didn't fit into this world, and maybe I didn't either.

She took my hand and squeezed it, and we continued to walk in silence.

After a while longer, holding hands wasn't enough for me, I felt a distance, and so I put my arm around her shoulder, and I held her close to me as we walked, and she snuggled in with a little whimper, and we walked, both of us looking straight ahead, both of us lost in our thoughts.

Sienna Rowe.

Zara.

They consumed me, consumed my mind.

Why had Sienna died?

How had Sienna died?

I guessed I would never know the whole truth.

I just hoped it was the only truth I would never find out, that now things would go back to normal, better than normal, I hoped it would go back to before "Oh boo," before Zara arrived even, so I could see her walk in again, stand at the front of the room, looking down, and then she could look up with those eyes and I would be lost again.

But I didn't want to go back there again either, because to go back there would be to miss all the time we had spent together, and with what had happened to Sienna, I wanted to keep every moment I had had with her ever.

I wanted all of her, and I wanted to give her all of me.

She kept walking but pulled away from my arm, and took my hand again, the cold surging through me, icier than ever before. Her eyes were ice too, blue ice, freezing me.

Without looking at me, without breaking stride, she spoke.

'The storm is coming, Hunter. You can feel it, can't you.'

I nodded.

'I can smell it.'

'I know. I can too. That's because we are one, connected. You said on Day 30, after school, that you would do anything for me. I have to know if that's still true. I have to know that you're with me. All the way. When the storm hits, Hunter, it's going to destroy things, and I can't let it destroy me. Or you. We have to do this together. You have to be my ray of light in the storm. Are you with me, Hunter? All the way?'

I nodded, knowing I was nodding because there was nothing else I would ever have done.

I nodded, and my fate was sealed.

I was hers to do with as she pleased.

And that was exactly what she did.

Day 48

Monday.

School.

After Sienna had died the town was, as I had said, in a daze.

But now, on Monday, at school, it was suddenly a whirl of action and activity, the winds picking up, the drops of rain still coming at long intervals, but heavy, and getting closer together.

In the distance, lightning was crashing, thunder rumbling gently, but warning us of what was to come.

On Day 48, teachers didn't teach, not in their usual way, at least.

Not for the first hour, at least.

They gathered our entire year level for a special assembly.

Mr Gallagher sat and talked to us, explaining things, explaining that we would be feeling things, and that was okay.

Mr Osborne sat while Mrs Brewer and another lady, a psychologist, talked to us, explaining that we would be feeling things, and that was okay.

Miss Little sat and talked to us, explaining that we would be feeling things, and that was okay.

We sat and listened and felt things, and that was okay.

Apparently.

Then classes started up again, and things were back to normal.

Another Monday.

And for Zara, it was just like it had been after the dance, although slightly more subtle.

Sienna was gone, but Julie was relentless, her anger fueled by Sienna reaching out to Zara at the end.

This wasn't a time for open abuse now though, so Julie changed tact.

The mocking continued.

The teasing.

The whispers behind her back.

The words to her face when teachers left the room.

I asked her about it at lunch, as we sat at the table, Glenn and the others playing cards. We were holding hands and facing each other, and I asked her about it.

She smiled and said it was nothing she hadn't seen before, and she knew how to handle it now.

After the other times, she knew what was coming.

I hoped she did, because it wasn't just what they were doing and saying now, I knew they would be planning more.

Planning things to do to her.

Making up stories about her.

Lying.

Destroying.

And yet, somehow, although she'd seemed broken after the books were destroyed, now she seemed to be getting stronger.

I couldn't work out why.

Or how.

How she was doing it.

If it was all an act.

But she seemed to stand taller, and in front of Julie, the smile never left her face.

With every message or post she found out about, she seemed to smile more.

With every whisper, mocking her, she answered another question in class.

Julie was going insane.

She ramped up her efforts.

Nothing worked.

Zara was invincible.

Incredible.

It was like she was wanting them to do it, like every bad word spoken was life to her.

It was like she wanted them to do more, to build up, for it to get worse.

She wanted them to try and destroy her.

It was like that, but I knew that couldn't be right.

Who would *want* that?

The only thing that gave her away were her eyes.

There was no blue anymore.

They had turned grey, and they hadn't turned back.

And I knew the gentle rumbling in the distance would soon become a roar.

And then I didn't know what would happen.

Mum, when I got home, sat and listened to me, but there was nothing to listen to.

So she spoke.

'Hunter, how are you feeling about this? I know you

weren't friends with Sienna, but still.'

I said nothing.

What could I say?

Was I glad she was dead?

No, not at all.

Was I glad it was one less person to bully Zara?

Hell yes, I was.

'Will you go to the funeral?'

I looked at her. I hadn't thought about that. The teachers had told us the funeral would be the following day, and that we could all have the afternoon off to go to it.

I stared at Mum, who analysed me for a moment and then nodded.

'You don't have to go,' she said.

'No,' I said, speaking for the first time. 'I do. I have to.'

It felt like it would be closure.

Little did I know, it would actually be an opening, and that the third crack would be the widest of all.

Day 49

Sienna's funeral.

We left school at 1, so we could go home and change and then head to the funeral.

I left with Zara. She walked with me to my house, holding my hand, swinging my arm gently.

And she talked the whole way.

The whole way home, she talked, and I honestly have no idea what she was saying, and I didn't care, because the sound of her voice, the rise and fall, that was enough.

If I could hear her, I knew I was okay.

I knew *she* was okay.

And that was all that mattered.

At my door, she spun me around and held me.

'Oh Hunter,' she said, holding me as if it was the last time she would ever do so. 'Sienna dying, it is so sad. So sad. But it was her time. That's what happens. We all have our time, and this was hers. Right?'

I didn't know what to say, so I said nothing.

'But today will be beautiful. It will celebrate her life, and who she was. It will bring closure for her family.'

I said nothing.

She kissed my neck and then broke off the hug.

'And,' she said, a cheeky smile on her face, 'I know you will look super handsome in a suit. See you soon.'

She kissed me quickly, and then she was gone.

I stood there, watching her walk off, and wondering how she could be like that, how she could switch to light and cheery even amongst the bullying, even with Sienna's death a grey cloud over us.

But that was what she did.

And what I did was go inside and change into the one suit I had, and then Mum drove me to the funeral.

It was packed, when we arrived. I saw Glenn, who came over to me, and we stood together, watching the parade of people.

Schoolfriends, family, sports teammates, people from her dance school, Sienna had been well-loved by everyone.

'Look at Hunter's little heart breaking!'

I shut my eyes and shook my head, trying to clear her voice out of my mind, not wanting to remember that, not today, today was about Sienna and it was about remembering the good things.

The good things.

'Where's Zara?' Glenn asked as we watched the last people file into the church. I shrugged, acting casual.

'She said she'd be here.'

'I gotta go in. I'll save you both a seat.'

I nodded. Glenn was such a good friend. I needed that.

I waited as long as I could, but she didn't arrive.

Someone asked if I was coming in, as they were about to close the doors and start the service.

I scanned the world one last time, but she wasn't there, she wasn't coming.

I guessed this was her statement.

This was her saying, 'You treat me like that, I won't pay you any respects.'

No.

Surely not.

I breathed in deeply, let it out, put my hands in my pockets and went inside to sit with Glenn, a spare seat next to me, obvious to everyone who it was for, obvious to everyone that she wasn't there.

The service began.

Family talked, the pastor talked, friends talked, and then Julie got up to speak.

For everything she was, everything she did, there was no denying Julie was beautiful, and when she stood up there, dressed in black, tears in her eyes, her face actually gentle, she looked stunning.

And when she started to speak, when she spoke with tenderness of her friend, and how she missed her, and how hard it was going to be without her, the room listened without a breath.

No one could take their eyes off her.

No one wanted to.

Until the doors opened.

Julie stopped, mid-sentence, and she stared.

'No,' she said, her voice shaking. 'No. No no no no no.'

We all spun around to where she was looking, and the room gasped as one.

Sienna stood in the doorway, only it wasn't Sienna.

It was Zara.

Only it wasn't Zara.

It was Zara as Sienna, wearing Sienna's clothes, her hair done like Sienna wore hers, make-up like Sienna.

She had transformed herself into Sienna.

And she looked incredible.

She walked down the centre of the church, turning to smile at me as she went past our aisle, and then she was back in character.

She reached the front and went to the coffin, standing over it, hunching her shoulders now, and we knew she was crying, even though we could only see her back.

She stayed there for a while, and no one had spoken, not even Julie.

We all just watched.

Finally, she breathed in deep, stood up tall, and went to Julie, grabbing her and holding her tight for a long time.

She let go and turned to face us, her make up now running down her face, her eyes red, her hair slightly off-kilter, slightly not right.

She reached across and took Julie's hand. Julie was in shock, no idea how to react to this, no idea what to do, and her hand was taken. Zara lifted it, and kissed it, and then held onto it as she spoke.

'Sienna is gone,' she said. 'Sienna is gone, but she will never leave us. Today, I have dressed like her, and I feel her with me, but this is just an outer shell. This is for me to get to know her more, to feel her more. But you all know her already. You know what she was like, what she was *really* like. You know who she was, what she was capable of, what she could have been in this world.'

She spun her words on a loom, and although I knew what she was saying with each sentence, although I knew what the message was, all anyone else saw was the finished piece.

Except Julie.

She knew.

And she was hiding her anger.

'See, I only knew Sienna a short time, and I knew her from the outside. The hair, the makeup, the clothes, the beauty, and that's all I can recreate. But there was so much more. *She* was so much more. You all knew her heart, and she had a strong heart, she had a heart that let her down, but it is one that will never break if you all keep a hold of it in your own. And not just in your hearts. Keep her wherever you can.'

She looked around the room, and as she spoke, her eyes fell on different people.

On Ashleigh.

'In your guts, your central being.'

On Archie.

'In your soul.'

On me.

'In the one you love.'

On Marcus.

'Behind your eyes, so you can see her always.'

On Tracey.

'Somewhere safe, so she will never be torn away from you.'

And finally she turned to Julie.

'Feel her everywhere, Julie. She was yours, your friend, and at the end she was with you, so if you feel her with your entire being, if you feel her everywhere, she will never go away, it will never stop, the love you have for her.'

She hugged Julie again and I looked around the room, and saw people nodding, wiping at their eyes, holding each other.

I looked back to the front.

She was still holding Julie, but now she let go and walked towards me.

Her words had touched people's hearts. *She* had touched people' hearts. She had made it a day to remember, to celebrate Sienna.

So why had my entire body turned to ice?

Day 50

Wednesday.

Not everything went on as normal.

Everything had changed.

As soon as Julie and Zara were in the same room, electricity charged the air. Julie wasn't even trying to hide it now, she was red and black and anger and hardness.

Zara was pastel blues and greys, but still those eyes.

Those eyes.

Every time Zara answered a question, Julie would comment.

Every time Julie answered a question, Julie would comment.

Julie would comment on everything.

We were all swept up in the whirlwind, we were all caught in the storm, in danger of being washed away, depending on whose side we chose.

In English, we had to give an oral presentation. The topic was space.

Julie stood up.

'I'd like to go first please, Miss Little.'

'Of course, Julie, but only if you feel up to it. We all know what …'

She couldn't even finish the sentence.

Julie didn't care. She walked to the front of the room.

She had a piece of paper in her hand. For all her faults, Julie was a great writer. She knew how to get to the heart of things, and she knew deepness, and she knew what the teachers liked.

But not today.

Today, it was a thinly disguised attack.

'It came, one day, from its world, to a world of peace.

It came, and it changed everything.

It thought it was one of us, it thought it could fit in, but we knew different.

It thought it was innocent, it thought it was nice, but we knew different.

We knew it was only a matter of time.

We knew that we would give it a chance, we would do all we could,

but that, in the end
It
Was
Different.
And it
Didn't
Want
To
Be
One
Of
Us.
It wanted to change us, to make us like it,
To draw us in, lead us on, take our hearts and then
Once we were in its world
It would turn
Only, it didn't know something
It didn't know about us, our strength,
Our numbers.
It didn't know that even if one of us falls, that only strengthens the
rest
It only makes it worse for it, because now, we are united.
Now we are one.
Now it is in our world, and there is only one solution.
It cannot be in our world any longer.
It
Can
Not
Be.
Because if it stays, if it continues to infect us, if it continues to bleed
us dry, our strength will build
And it will die
It has a chance to go, to escape, to be free, to find another world
But the door is closing, and once it does, once we and it and us and
it are locked in this world

She finished. The whole time she had read the poem, she hadn't looked at the paper.

She had memorised it and had been staring straight at Zara, who had been watching, rapt, focused, locked in.

As soon as Julie said the last word, everyone clapped, as we had been trained to do, but most clapped because they understood.

I also understood.

I clapped because I was a trained seal.

Zara was on her feet, tears in her eyes, smiling as she clapped.

'Julie, oh Julie!' she said, her voice easily heard above the applause of the class, then before anyone could breathe, while the clapping continued, she ran to the front of the room and, just like at the funeral, she hugged Julie, whose arms stayed straight at her sides. Zara hugged her and she wouldn't let go, and then she finally did, and she returned to her seat, everything but her eyes showing how much she had loved that poem, how much she hadn't understood it had been about her, how much she had been so pleased for Julie.

Everything but her eyes.

And her eyes spoke of revenge.

Day 51

The whirlwind had me, and it wouldn't let me out. Every moment at school on Day 51 was spent wondering what was going to happen, wondering who was going to strike next, what her revenge would be when it came.

And I had seen those eyes.

Revenge *would* come.

But the worst thing was … nothing happened.

There was no strike, there was no retaliation, there was nothing.

And that was the worst thing of all.

I look back now, and I wonder if I had done something on Day 51, if I had somehow changed the day, if it would have been different.

But I didn't, and it wasn't, and so after school, on Day 51, when it began, I was right there by Zara's side.

No.

That's a lie.

She was right there by my side, because when the next blow was struck, it wasn't by Zara, or Julie, or Ashleigh, or Archie, or even Glenn.

It wasn't anyone logical.

The first blow was struck by me.

The whirlwind had me, and it wouldn't let me out.

Day 51 – After School

I didn't say goodbye to anyone at school. Not on Day 51. I picked my books up, I grabbed my bag, and I was out the door.

I saw her watching me, her eyes trying to draw me in, but I looked away and I walked.

I had to get out of there.

I didn't know what was coming, but I knew something was and I was scared and I needed space.

I didn't get it.

Halfway home, as I reached into my bag to get my drink, I felt a scrunched up piece of paper, and when I opened it, and read it, my heart stopped.

The storm is here. The first rain has fallen, and we are about to feel the full force of nature. Things have changed now. I know you said you would be with me, but are you still? All the way?

As soon as I stopped reading, as soon as I looked up from the paper, she was there, in front of me, her eyes searching for an answer I wouldn't consciously give, but that was there for her to see.

I knew it wouldn't have mattered how well I had hidden it, she would have seen it anyway.

Of course I was with her.

I was always with her.

No matter how scared I was, no matter what I saw in those eyes, I wanted nothing else but her.

Without a word, she took the paper and put it in my bag, then she held my hand and we walked. As we did, she leant her head on my shoulder, and I closed my eyes, trusting her to lead me, breathing her in, all of her, feeling her essence seep into my being.

Her head shifted slightly, and her lips brushed my ear as she spoke.

'Can you meet me later?'

I was going to say I wasn't allowed out at night, but I knew that wouldn't fly. Couldn't fly. I had spent the night with her on Day 39.

And besides, I *wanted* to be there with her. I *wanted* to be her ray of light in the storm. I didn't know what Julie had planned next, or what Zara knew had planned for that matter, but I knew the stakes had been raised, and I knew I had to be there.

I hadn't even answered, but I felt her smile and her head returned to my shoulder, and I could feel her satisfaction.

'Good, Hunter. It's so good. I'll see you at 11.'

She let go of my hand.

'Where?' I asked, finally opening my eyes, but when I did, when I looked around, she was gone.

And I had never felt so small and alone.

Day 51 – Rumblings

Thunderstorms, when they hit, are scary and exciting and glorious all at once. Lightning is artwork in the sky, and thunder, rolling in, slowly, and then, every now and then, crashing, feels like a warning to the world.

A warning of what is possible.

In the distance, a thunderstorm is incredible.

When that storm is right above you, when the thunder isn't rolling in, but is crashing out of the anticipation, and the windows shake and animals run for cover, and you scream and then laugh nervously to pretend that you weren't scared at all, but your eyes betray you, your thumping heart betrays you, that is when you realise you are powerless, that when the storm hits, when nature shows even a fraction of its full power, that despite what you think, despite how strong you think you are, despite how much you think you want to be there, there are forces out there that can destroy without blinking. With a flick of their finger, they can have you at their mercy, crush you whenever they like.

The thunder had been rolling for a while now, since the books being torn, since the confrontations in class, lightning flashing in the distance, the smell in the air that told you a storm was coming.

There had been the drops too, the spread out drops of rain, drop … drop … drop.

We all waited, but not many of us knew what we were waiting for.

In the past, there had been drops, but then the storm would pass by us, not causing us direct damage.

Avril leaving, that was a storm passing us, destroying something beautiful that we were no longer connected to.

Zara didn't leave.

We were still connected.

I was still connected.

When the storm came, this time I was in the middle of it.

No.

I *was* it.

She came to me at 11pm, on Day 51.

Tap tap tap on the window.

Once in my room, we hugged, no, not hugged, when she held me, leaping at me and grabbing on, it was like we were in the storm and the wind was blowing, and I was her rock, holding her in, keeping her in the one place.

I was her rock.

Oh my God, I was her rock.

I held her as tight as I could, breathing her in, wishing for her to say we would go to her place, that was what this was about, relishing the coolness her body gave mine now, longing for it.

She released the hug and stared at me for a minute, searching, then her face broke into a grin I had never seen before, but one I wanted to see always.

It was a smile I knew was only for me.

Her eyes narrowed, and she looked around conspiratorially.

'It's a dark night, Hunter,' she said, her voice parodying the old spy movies. 'It's a dark night full of mystery, and here we are, adventure ahead of us, two old school heroes against the world. It's us against them, and them ain't got a chance!'

Only she could turn a moment like this into something fun.

The storm may have been coming, but I was protected from it.

The bubble held me close and felt like it would never pop.

Day 51 – The Storm

We walked, as usual, and everything felt normal.

Until we arrived at Ashleigh's house, and stood across the street from it, watching.

I knew it was Ashleigh's. I'd been to a party there.

It had been third grade.

I'd never been here since, and I didn't know why we were here now.

Or maybe I did.

This was the revenge.

Zara wasn't going straight for Julie.

She wasn't that obvious.

Cold seeped into my veins.

'Why are we here?' I asked.

She didn't answer, she just kept staring at the house across the street, the house in darkness, people sleeping unaware. I looked at her, my question hanging in the air like a skeleton in the closet. I spun her to me, made her look at me.

'Why are we here?' I asked again, staring into her eyes, the grey lighting up everything in me.

'Because you are going to help me, Hunter, like you said you would. It starts tonight. The storm is here. The storm is now.'

Thunder, lightning, rain, wind.

'There's a theory,' she said, 'in battle, that you take out the leader first, and the rest will then crumble. But that seems too easy, too fast, too blah. To me, Hunter, what they did to me, what they …'

She suddenly grabbed me, holding my arms tight at the shoulder, her eyes a flash of green, deep sea green for an instant, then back to grey, but still she held me underwater.

'Do you love me?' she asked, her voice a million miles away.

'Hunter! Do you love me?'

I nodded. I did. Despite the chill that was in me, despite the feeling that everything was about to change, I *did* love her, I loved her totally and completely and I felt it now, rushing through me, a warmth of love I had never felt while her hands were on me, while we were in contact before, I felt warmth rush through me and now she was underwater with me, and we were swimming, and the water swirled around us, everything a blur, frosted, there but not there, and the only thing that was clear was her, and she was crystal clear, her outline so sharp it almost hurt to look at, her scarf swirling now, and suddenly part of it lifted and I didn't see underneath it but I saw her face, I saw it change, darken, and then the scarf was back and she was Zara again, and she was love and she was life.

Life.

She gave me life.

We swirled and we turned and she held me when it felt like I was going too far under, and she made me stable, strong, firm, able to do whatever she asked, able to survive anything, and then we were on the lawn, at Ashleigh's house, the water a dream, and I was on my knees, and she was there, holding me, whispering in my ear, thanking me, stroking my neck, my hair, crying into my shoulder, telling me it was alright, it would all be alright, we had each other, and that would always be enough, and I held her, so close, one body, one soul, and it was only when she let go and stood, only when I watched her turn, that I saw blood all over her back.

Blood that had come from my hands.

And when I went to scream, when my lungs opened, she was there, and the scream never came.

Day 52

I avoided her at school. I avoided her like the plague, as they say.

"They."

It wasn't Glenn's they".

But it wasn't mine either.

It didn't matter.

Because when I arrived at school, the only "they" that mattered was Ashleigh, and Ashleigh was dead.

No.

Not just dead.

Torn apart, like someone had reached into her and ripped out her insides.

Gutted.

And there was only one connection to that word I could

make, and that was Zara.

'Look at her, she's gutted!' Ashleigh had said.

Look at Ashleigh.

She's gutted.

'Look at Hunter's little heart breaking.'

'Look at her, she's gutted.'

First Sienna, then Ashleigh.

As always, at schools, the rumours spread.

She had been killed in her bed.

She had been attacked by a wild animal.

She had been raped by a wild animal.

Kids, when their imagination allows it, will dream up anything and everything.

My imagination was running wild, because I had to pretend it was imagination, I had to convince myself it was imagination.

She had helped me get the blood off my hands before taking me home.

After she left I had gotten into bed, but I hadn't slept.

I lay there, frosted images clouding my mind, looking at my hands, so clean, so clear, and I wondered if anything had happened at all.

Then I got to school, and I heard Ashleigh had died.

No.

Ashleigh had been ripped apart.

There was another special assembly, and I sat with Glenn, and that was it.

There was no Zara.

She hadn't come to school.

I thought of her eyes, of her smell, of everything about her.

I thought of how I had imagined her scarf lifting, of the darkness, but I pushed it all away.

I was losing my mind.

I was in love, and I was scared, and I was twisting everything so I could leave again, leave her to face them like I'd done with Avril.

Zara was no killer.

Zara wasn't evil.

I was evil, thinking like this.

I was evil.

I was going to leave her alone, no ray of light, and all because I was imagining things that weren't possible.

Had she hypnotised me somehow with her eyes, made me kill Ashleigh?

Even the thought of it was ridiculous.

The thought that she could do that, the thought that I could do that.

It was ridiculous, a dream.

There had been no blood on my hands when I was home, in bed.

Nothing.

My clothes had been clean, my skin had been clean, my conscience was clean.

Whoever had killed Ashleigh, however it had been done, I had been a part of it, and no matter how many times I thought that, I still didn't believe it.

'Hunter!'

Glenn's voice snapped my out of wherever I was. He was looking at me, worried.

'Dude, what's going on? Where were you? It's done. They're finished.'

I stared at him, and I knew my eyes betrayed what I knew to be true.

I knew it hadn't been a dream.

It had happened.

I had killed her.

We had killed her.

And not only that, I knew we would do it again.

Day 53

We.

A word that brings thoughts of togetherness, of love, of skipping through the park.

We.

For me, we had always been a dream, unattainable, a far-off land.

There was I at home, and there was I with my friends, and there was I at school.

But there had never been a we.

Not even with Avril Matthews.

Perhaps there could have been, but there wasn't.

Because of me.

Because of me, there was no we.

But now there was we, and it scared me so much that I wanted to scream, '***WHERE AM I? WHERE HAVE I GONE? WHO IS THIS BODY I NOW INHABIT? WHERE AM I?***'

At first, the we had been amazing, obviously.

I had been swept off my feet, and I had allowed myself to be swept.

I had loved it.

I had loved her.

I *still* loved her.

So much.

But now, after Sienna, and especially after Ashleigh, it had changed.

But not in the way I had thought it would.

My love became a yearning, a longing, a desire to have her back, to have the old Zara back.

The one who didn't kill.

But it also became a yearning and a longing for that moment where we had been on Ashleigh's lawn, or so I had thought, because in that moment, in that feeling of being underwater, in that moment of frosted glass and swirling water, I had never felt more connected to another human being.

I had never been so we.

I didn't know if I would ever feel that again.

But I knew I wanted to, and if you want to talk about a feeling scaring you, well that feeling, that feeling of wanting that connectivity, but also knowing what it would mean, that scared me to death, and made me think that perhaps death was the only option, the only way to save the others.

Day 55

Ashleigh's funeral.

Again, I went.

I went because I felt like I had to, like I had to be there, because if I didn't go, people would know.

They would suspect and they would know and they would come to my house, everyone, from the funeral, and they would point and they would say, 'We know.'

And they would take me away and they would exact revenge, revenge that would be deserved.

If I had actually done it.

So I had to go.

I had to be there.

And I *wanted* to be there, I wanted to be there with Zara.

I hadn't spoken to her since the night Ashleigh had died, hadn't felt her near me, hadn't smelt her.

I missed pasted blues and greys.

I missed them so much.

So I put on my suit, unworn for so long, now twice in a week, and I went.

The funeral felt different to Sienna's.

For starters, it wasn't Sienna, the girl who never got sick.

This was Ashleigh.

Not that Ashleigh got sick a lot, that came out wrong, it was just … this was Ashleigh.

If Julie was number one, perfection in the eyes of most people, and Sienna was perfection in health, Ashleigh was perfection in ways almost beyond her control.

She was the usual mean girl story – rich family, not super bright but gorgeous, not quite perfect but close enough to be above 99% of the rest of the school, the town, but always destined to be number two … or, in her eyes, number three after what Julie had said at Sienna' s funeral.

That had almost killed her, I had seen it.

That had almost killed her.

I almost laughed out loud, catching myself just in time.

Laughing at a funeral of the girl I had … I caught myself from thinking that as well, but I could feel eyes on me.

I could feel people watching, and where was Zara? Would she make a grand entrance again?

People were thinking that too, wondering that, it was obvious, and that was why they were looking at me.

Hunter will know, they thought. Hunter does everything with her, spends every possible moment with her, kills people with her.

'You okay?'

Glenn.

Solid, trustworthy, noble Glenn.

You're too good for me.

I don't deserve you. Not as a friend, not as a person I speak to, not as anything, but here you are, dependable Glenn, always there, backing me up, the strong one, the defender of the weak, always Glenn, Glenn, *GLENN!*

'Yeah. Thanks, Glenn. This is just kind of full on, ya know?'

Glenn nodded, but looked at me slightly differently to normal.

'It's just, you're sweating. You might be sick. If you're getting sick, you have to get it checked out, Hunter, after what happened to …'

Sienna.

I thought it for him.

I thought the words.

He hadn't been going to say Ashleigh.

Sickness doesn't gut you like a hunter's catch.

Oh Jesus.

A Hunter.

I rubbed my temples.

'I actually don't feel great,' I said. 'Might need to sit down.'

Glenn took my arm and led me inside, to a seat.

Where was Zara?

I needed her.

Now.

I needed her there with me, and not just because I needed her wanted her longed for her, I needed her there so people could stare at *her* and stop staring at *me*, eyes boring into me, asking questions, all the time questions.

I sat down and Glenn sat next to me.

'You better get back out there, Glenn. I'll be fine.'

'Dude. You look like crap. I'm not leaving you unless it's to get you an ambulance.'

'Maybe some water?' I asked.

I had to be alone.

I needed to be alone, away from the eyes, the stares, the questions.

He nodded and left, telling me not to go anywhere while he was gone.

Not to die while he was gone.

Dying at a funeral.

Ha!

Well, it would make the arrangements a lot easier.

I laughed at my own joke.

'It's nice to see you smile, Hunter. I've missed it. I've missed you.'

I jumped, and turned, and she was there, on the bench, a few spots down from me. I hadn't heard or seen her come in, but I had been in my own little world, making jokes at a funeral.

At Ashleigh's funeral.

She slid along a little, head tilted, analysing me, but not like the others. Not like everyone outside. Not with questions.

She slid a little more.

'You don't look so good,' she said, only a metre between us now.

I wanted her touch. I wanted her next to me, brushing against me, sending chills through me, and yet now there was something else, something that was making me not want it as well.

'You don't look so good,' she repeated, sliding closer again. Half a metre.

She turned slightly, and pastel blues and greys touched me, and I closed my eyes and breathed it in, feeling it fill me, feeling it give me everything I needed, and when I breathed out and opened my eyes, she was right there, right next to me, her arm curled through mine, her fingers stroking my hand, her head on my shoulder, and she was saying that this time, this funeral, she wasn't speaking, she wasn't leaving this seat, wasn't leaving me, that I wouldn't have to go through this on my own, that she was there, always, and that it was we now, not us, we, and it would always be we, people would always know it was we, Hunter and Zara, always.

Till death do us part.

Glenn came back with water, and he started when he saw Zara, I noticed it.

'Hey,' he said, composing himself. 'Didn't see you come in.'

She smiled at him, crooked smile, perfect smile.

'I snuck past while you were getting the water, talking to the people.'

Glenn nodded and handed me the water, which I took and drank, but I didn't miss the look on his face as he gave it to me, the look of yes, he had been talking to people, but that was just as easy to guess as to see.

People started filing into the church.

They looked at us as they walked in, well, looked at her,

wondering what she would do, if she would talk like she had at Sienna's, if she would upstage Julie.

Like she had at Sienna's.

She didn't even seem to notice they were there.

She didn't look, didn't move, apart from snuggling even closer into me, her head, her body, everything, like she wanted to be inside of me, be a part of me.

Like she wasn't already.

The service started and it was the usual, but always I felt their eyes, always I knew they were looking at me. The people up the front talking, the people in the crowd, all turning at some point to look at me, not all at the same time, but eventually they all would.

Every person who spoke, they seemed to be directing their words at me.

'Terrible end to a beautiful life.'

'Who would want to ruin something so perfect?'

'Why Ashleigh? Why not someone else. Why Ashleigh?'

Every word, every look, every breath.

My heart was racing.

Zara tried to soothe me, rubbing my arm, nuzzling in closer, but every word, every look, why didn't anyone else notice they were staring at me?

Why didn't Glenn do his usual thing, defend me, stand up, tell them to stop, ask them what their problem was, why were they staring at his friend, what was wrong with them, we were here to mourn Ashleigh, not to accuse Hunter.

Accuse Hunter.

Of what?

I laughed, a short, sharp bark, quiet, but loud enough for everyone around to hear.

'Hunter, baby, shush.'

Zara.

Baby.

I looked up the front, realised I hadn't actually looked up

there for a while now, seen who was speaking, and it was Julie, always Julie, of course it was Julie when I had laughed, and her eyes and the eyes of everyone else bored into me, asking questions, every stare a question, where was I on the night of Day 51, what had I been doing, did I kill her?

My stomach swirled and she held me, sensing what was going on, somehow as always in me, part of me, knowing everything about me, telling me I didn't have to be strong, she would be strong for me, she would hold me up, that they weren't looking, Hunter, they're not looking at you, it's okay, you're just imagining things, look at me, Hunter look at me now please Hunter please but I couldn't look, no matter how much I wanted to, because a part of me suddenly feared what I would see, that it wouldn't be her, not the her I knew, it would be someone or something else, I couldn't look but I looked and she was there, and her eyes caught me and held me and I had never felt such love, such love in cold steel grey eyes, not a trace of blue, nothing, but they held me and I felt safe and then suddenly I heard a scream, a scream, a scream, and I couldn't stay in those eyes anymore, she had done it again, hypnotised me and I had done something I knew I had but I didn't know what, so I stood and I climbed out of the seat and I ran, and Glenn called after me but I ran, I ran out of that church and I didn't stop running until now my heart was screaming and my throat was scorched and I fell to the ground, the concrete path tearing at my clothes, my skin, and then I crawled to the grass, and I didn't know where I was.

Until I lay on the grass, and I looked up, and I saw it.

I saw the house.

I was at Zara's.

Day 56

I sat in the waiting room at the psychologist.

Mum was with me, reading a magazine, playing it cool, but I knew what she was thinking.

We're back again. When will he be okay? Is it my fault?

*Should I have done something different? Running out of a funeral? Maybe he **is** crazy.*

I looked around the room, feeling eyes on me, feeling questions. I wished Zara was there, holding my hand, nuzzling into me, like she had done at the funeral.

The funeral.

When she had come to me, outside her house, finding me lying there, arriving not long after I had, somehow, *how had she done that*, had she run after me, she lay next to me, holding me close, rocking me, telling me this was normal, this was what happened, this was such a hard situation and that it was going to be okay.

She talked as if it was about Ashleigh and Sienna dying, but inside I knew it was more than that.

It wasn't just about them dying.

She told me that what had happened, outside Ashleigh's that night, it had bonded us, joined us even more than before, that now she knew I would do anything, and that she needed to know that, because the storm wasn't over, it was just beginning.

This was just the start.

Soon the winds would come.

And then she had held me and soothed me and whispered love into my being, and we had lay there for a long time, until the dew seeped into our clothes and the chill seeped into our bones, and I had stood then, and so had she, and we had held each other some more, and she had whispered in my ear, 'That was some scream you did.'

I stepped back, stared at her.

I did?

I screamed?

Me?

That had been me*?*

She had smiled at me then, realising, and she had held me close and whispered more words, but I didn't hear anything, all I could hear was that scream, that scream I had thought had come from the front, from someone else, from someone I had ... but I hadn't! I hadn't! I hadn't I hadn't I hadn't.

Oh happy day!

I hugged her close, oh God I loved her so much, and I had run home, suddenly light again, suddenly feeling free, suddenly knowing that maybe I was imagining things, maybe my thoughts were running away from me, but I wasn't a killer.

She wasn't hypnotising me.

If I was just a little crazy, that I could handle.

So now, here I was.

At the psychologist's.

And I was ready to talk.

I sat in the chair, staring at the psych. I had thought I was ready to talk, but as soon as I was in there, as soon as I started telling her about Zara, about how I felt, she held her hands up, smiling, her mouth smiling, and she said we would get to that, that there were other things we needed to discuss first.

That we needed to go back before we could discuss now.

NO!

Now was what mattered.

Now was what was happening and it didn't matter what had happened before, well it did, of course it did, but now was now and why couldn't I talk about Zara, about how she made me feel, about Zara?

But we didn't.

She didn't want to.

So she asked questions about Sienna and Ashleigh and how it made me feel, them dying, and did it bring back any memories, did it make me feel more like talking, but it didn't, it had but it didn't now, so I grunted replies, and she said that she wanted to help me, she really did, but that I had to help myself too, I had to help her, and the only way we could do that was by talking things out, getting them out into the open, and then we could change my thoughts, change the thoughts that were making me feel bad and turn them into good thoughts.

And she had smiled at me with her mouth.

Zara appeared then, in the room, and I knew it wasn't actually her but it was enough. She sat in a chair, behind the psych, and she smiled at me with everything she had, and I felt her, from across the room, I felt her hold me up, and I felt myself sit taller in the chair, and with that tiny movement, suddenly I felt more confident, more alive, and I smiled.

'I'm ready to talk,' I said.

'Oh Hunter, that's wonderful, I mean, we don't have a lot of time left, but this, even you saying this, is a wonderful start. Tell me then, what would you like to say?'

'There's a girl,' I said. 'Zara.'

'Oh, Hunter,' she sighed. 'We talked about this. We need to discuss other things, other times. Avril. Sienna. Ashleigh. Then we can talk about Zara.'

'No,' I said, hands gripping the armrest. 'You don't understand. All of them, all of that, it only matters because of Zara. She's the *only* thing that matters. The only thing.'

'I have to go, Hunter,' Zara said. I heard her. The psych didn't. Go? What?

Zara smiled at me, nodding, playing with her scarf, and I caught the faintest scent of her, pastel blues touching my nostrils. I could tell them apart now the blues and greys.

I could tell everything apart.

'Now?' I said, knuckles gripping the armrest, tension returning.

'No, Hunter,' the psych said. 'Another time.'

'I can't stay, Hunter, not with them. Not with all of them trying to destroy us. I can't let them hurt you.'

'What? Me?'

'Yes, it's all you, but I said another time, Hunter. Today is for talking about the past. We must clear that up before you can have a future.'

'Hunter, I have to protect you, but if you want me to stay,

if you *really* want me to stay ...'

'Yes! I really do.'

'Yes, Hunter,' the psych said. 'You do. You have to clear out the past. That's the only way.'

'There's only one way, Hunter.'

'Only one way?'

The two conversations were overlapping, merging into one, until I didn't know who was saying what and who I was speaking to.

'You can't go,' I said. 'Not now. Not when-'

'Now is the only time, my love. I have to go now. I can't stay anymore.'

'It has to be now, Hunter. If not now, when? When will you be ready to talk about the past?'

'You have to stay!'

'We're almost out of time.'

'Almost out of time.'

'No. Now! Don't you see?'

'I see *you*,' Zara said, reaching out for me. '*I* see you, Hunter. Only me.'

'I do,' the psych said in her maddeningly controlled and calming and practised voice. 'I really do, Hunter, and eventually you will be happy, but we aren't here to talk about your happiness right now.'

Are you kidding me?

Did she actually just say that?

'We're not?'

'We are, baby. We're going to be so happy.'

'No, Hunter, not yet. We will, I promise you, we'll change the thoughts, but we need to go deeper first, we need to find the thoughts that are hurting you.'

I looked away from Zara. I had to. I focused on the real person.

'But nothing hurts me when I'm with her. Don't you get it? Don't you get that if we talk about her we will find my happiness?'

'Not today, Hunter.'

Not ever.

I stood out of my chair.

Zara stepped towards me.

The psych stood too.

'Hunter? We still have a minute.'

No.

We don't.

We're done.

There's only one person worth talking about, only one person worth talking to, and it isn't you, lady. If you don't want to talk about Zara, we don't want to talk to you.

I smiled at Zara, over the psych's shoulder, and then I turned and left.

Mum looked up, shocked, as I walked out of the room and past her. She checked her watch, then saw the Psych staring helplessly after me.

'That was great, Mum,' I said as I walked out of the office. 'So helpful. It made me see what's important to me.'

And then I walked to the car and waited for her, for Zara, and I saw her running up to me, sprinting to me, and holding me like she wanted to feel my soul, saying she was so proud of me, that I didn't need to talk things out, not with them, I could talk to her, I *would* talk to her, I just needed to be and do, and that if I did that, if I trusted her, if I did what she wanted, we would be together, and we would make things right.

Make me right.

Make me whole.

But I already was.

I already *was* whole, when I was with her.

Everyone else, Julie, Archie, the psychologist, they were planning against me, trying to hold me back, trying to break me, break Zara, break us, but they couldn't.

Not now.

Not after this.

I looked at her as Mum came out to the car, and I nodded.

I was in.

All the way.

Ashleigh's yard, feeling underwater, feeling connected, despite what may or may not have happened, perhaps because of what may or may not have happened, I wanted that again.

And I wanted it now.

Day 57

Now.

What time is now?

Does now even exist?

Does time even exist?

Does anything actually exist, or is it all something we have created in our minds? Is now for me different to now for someone else, or are we all operating on the same now? How can now for me awake be the same as now for someone sleeping on the other side of the world? What is it and what does it all mean and what matters?

She matters.

Life doesn't just go on, not when she isn't in my now.

That's the only now that matters.

When I saw her standing there, waiting for me on Day 57, waiting outside our McDonalds, when I saw her there my heart didn't leap.

Everything leaped.

Leapt.

Grammar.

Doesn't matter.

She held me and I drowned in her. I let her smother me with everything she had.

'It's next level tonight,' she murmured. 'Are you up for it?'

I nodded into her.

Only her.

She was all that mattered, and the only other people that mattered were the ones trying to separate us, keep us apart.

Julie, Archie, Marcus, Tracey, Mum, the professionals.

They mattered.

They needed to not matter.

'Tracey first,' she whispered.

I nodded into her again.

'Do you remember what she said, on Day 42?'

Another nod.

'Tell me.'

I didn't speak. She broke off the hug, and hooked me with her eyes, grey beauty.

Steel death.

'Tear them apart,' I said.

'Tear them apart,' she repeated. 'You know what's happening, Hunter, don't you. You know what has to happen.'

It wasn't a question. It didn't need to be. She knew what I knew. She was in me. She *was* me.

Her hands slid down my arms and she took my hands in hers, and now they weren't just chilly, now they were freezing, pure ice, and she held my hands and I wanted to move, I found it hard to breath, but she had me, and she held me, and she wasn't letting go, and suddenly her hands weren't cold anymore, and heat surged through my body and I felt invincible, and then there we were, Tracey's house, and she massaged my hands, and she asked if I felt it, if I felt the cold and I said no and she laughed, she laughed and laughed and she didn't let go, and she asked me again and again I said no, I said her hands weren't cold anymore, and she laughed even more and then she kissed me, telling my mouth she loved me, saying the words into me so they swarmed through me, engulfed me, filled me until all I could see was her, just her and nothing else, just her and then I was there too, and I could see us and us and us and us and us and we kissed and it was like nothing else ever, it was like nothing else could ever be, no one could feel this, no one could love this deeply, and she held me and rocked me and stroked me and then there we were again, on a lawn, holding each other tight, only it wasn't a lawn this time, it was carpet, carpet in Tracey's room, and there was Tracey, on her bed, only it wasn't Tracey this time, it was what was left of Tracey after she had been torn open by a monster, a beast, something with strength and desire and coldness and singular vision, and the blood, everywhere the blood, over the sheets, the carpet, the walls, and Tracey, what was left of Tracey, eyes open, fear in her dead eyes like I had never seen, like she had been alive the whole time, watching, feeling, ripped open, torn apart, and I looked at Zara, pure, beautiful, amazing, clean, and then I looked down, and I saw, I saw, I saw that the beast, the monster, the killer that had torn Tracey apart, that killer was me, and Zara put her hands on my face and I recoiled, her hands ice again, and then I realised that it wasn't again at all, that they always had been ice, and that the only reason they had warmed me, the reason she had laughed, was not because she had become warmer, but because I had become colder, colder than even her, cold enough to do what I had done, to remove another person that mattered and just like at Ashleigh's it hit me, only this time I didn't scream, this time I didn't panic.

I was the storm now.

I was the rain and wind and thunder and lightning.

And I laughed.

I laughed from my soul, black as night, cold as ice.

And Zara laughed with me.

Day 58

We had left Tracey's after the laughter, after the feeling of cleansing.

That was what it felt like.

Cleansing.

Like I was cleansing our bubble of people trying to pop it, trying to destroy us.

That could never happen.

Only we mattered.

Nothing else.

Glenn called on Day 58, but I didn't answer. My mum called me down to breakfast, but I didn't go. I stayed in my room and I breathed in … everything.

Was this really me?

Was this who I had been, all this time? All this time of holding back, of letting others get away with everything, of leaving Avril to fight her own battles, had that been another me?

Or someone else?

Was this the real me after all?

Was that what she did? Was that what she was doing? Was she bringing the real me out, and was the real me a monster?

I started to worry then, the euphoria of the night before replaced by panic, sheer panic. My heart raced, I broke into a cold sweat, and I held onto the edge of the bed because I feared that if I let go, if I didn't hold on, that I would be sucked out of this world, ripped away from my mother, from Glenn, from her.

So I held on and I gritted my teeth, because I wasn't ready to go.

Not yet.

Our story wasn't done.

But the panic rose in me, making it hard to breathe, hard to do anything but hold on for dear life, waiting for it to pass, but it didn't pass and then just when I thought I was done for, when I thought I would scream, run, tell everyone everything, tell them what had happened, what was happening, tap … tap … tap.

The window.

Little stones.

I couldn't move.

I was holding myself on the bed but I was also holding the bed down, and I couldn't go, not yet, not when there were others, not when I needed this to stop or I would lose her and then she was there, she must have gone to the front door, and she was there, with me, wait, had the door opened, it didn't matter, she was on the bed, holding me, whispering in my ear again, her hair falling over my face, and I felt love wash through me, and it washed away everything else, and I could finally breathe again, I could finally release something out of my gut, and finally we lay there, and I relaxed, and she said to me that what I had done, for her, for us, what I had done was the right thing, that soon it would be okay, we would be free of them, free of everything, and so I smiled, and I closed my eyes, and I let her hold me, and I fell asleep.

Day 59

I couldn't see anymore. The storm had hit, and the rain was so strong, so heavy, sheets falling, that I couldn't see past anything.

I couldn't see past her.

I knew it was Day 59, but that was it. I didn't know what day of the week it was, if it was a school day, a weekend, I didn't know anything.

Well, that isn't entirely true.

I knew it was Day 59, and I knew it was the day of Tracey's funeral.

This time, I didn't go.

I couldn't go.

How could I? I would scream. I would laugh. I would do something, anything, that would give me away, give us away, take her away.

Take me away.

So I stayed in bed.

Mum came to the door, asked if I needed anything and in my mind I said yes, but I didn't speak out loud.

Eventually she went away.

Julie, Archie, Marcus.

They were all that remained.

Soon they would be gone too.

Gone.

I wondered if they knew, if anyone knew, if anyone realised.

It was so obvious.

Obvious to me, but I was in the storm, they were all in their houses, dry and safe, or so they thought, watching the storm, seeing the damage it caused, but holding on, staying safe, safe, safe.

They weren't safe.

How could they be?

How could they be safe from a force of nature?

How could they be safe from me?

I rolled over and faced the wall, although my eyes remained closed.

How had I done it? How had she made me do it?

What was she?

What was I?

I felt a presence behind me, and then she was there, arms around me, spooning me, pressing against me, and I was safe and dry, and even as the rain teemed down, sideways in the wind, I was safe and dry, and nothing could hurt me get to me stop me.

She was my bubble.

She was my heaven.

She was my hell.

'Tomorrow,' she whispered, 'we visit Archie.'

She was my hell.

She was my heaven.

She was my everything.

Day 60

Day 60. 60 days. Not even nine weeks. Not even two months. Not even a heartbeat, and yet it had been everything. I couldn't remember what life had been like before Day 1, before her head had risen and looked at the room, before I had seen those blue-grey eyes, before I had smelt her, felt her, been her.

Now, on Day 60, it was a new world. Not everyone from the old world had made it to Day 60, and not everyone would make it to Day 61. It was time to go next level.

I walked down the stairs at 9:45pm.

'Hi, Hunter,' Mum said, She was sitting at the kitchen table, waiting, I assume, for me, knowing I would go out, knowing I would see her.

Her.

Zara.

Her.

'Sit with me.'

I sat with her.

She played with her fingers, stroking one at a time, not looking at me, then finally she met my eyes.

'Hunter, I know you want to see Zara, I know you do, and I know how you feel about her but ...'

She sighed.

So did I, although it was more an intake of air. Did she know? Had she discovered something? Did she know what we had done? Was this the end?

'Hunter, there has been a curfew put in place. With what has been happening. It's a curfew for your own safety, for safety of all the children.'

Children.

Children.

Children.

Won't somebody think of the children?

'How late?' I asked, wondering how long I had.

'It's not just at night. School has been cancelled for the week while they conduct interviews. But you're also done for tonight, Hunter. It's a 9:30 curfew. It's for the safety of all the children.'

Interviews? About Tracey Ashleigh Sienna? This was it. This was the end. But I wasn't going to let her go down alone. I would stay with her until the end.

I breathed out and looked at Mum, playing it as cool as I

possibly could.

'Yeah you mentioned that, Mum. Thank you.'

She got out of her chair and walked around the table to me, dropping to her knees, taking her hands in mine, looking up at me.

'Please, Hunter. Please. I can't lose you. I can't. You're all I have left, and I need you here with me. It's so hard seeing you sad, but I know in time we can work this out, but not if you ... not if you aren't here. Please stay in. This week? Tonight? Please stay in?'

My mind raced, images of Zara, Mum, Archie, Ashleigh, all swirling, fighting for my attention, driving me this way and that.

I couldn't let Zara down.

I couldn't.

But my mother, staring up at me, her hands gripping mine, desperation in them, mothering in them, I had to stay.

And if I had to stay, I had to say no to Zara.

And right now, I couldn't handle doing that.

I wanted to yes everything she said and did, and saying no felt like breaking the loop.

Better to say nothing at all.

Or so I thought.

But I did think it, and so when I went to my room, when I slid under the sheets, my phone stayed on the floor.

And when it buzzed at me constantly, when it wouldn't let me be, I picked it up and I held it close to me, against my chest, every buzz ripping into me, punishment for ignoring it.

Every buzz pleading at me to be with her.

Every buzz screaming at me, 'Hunter! Please! Now! You said you were in it. You said you would do anything. You said you were my ray of light.'

But when I finally looked, when I finally read the messages, they didn't say any of those things.

They didn't say anything at all.

In fact, it was just one picture, over and over and over and over again, and that picture was a before and after photo of Archie.

Before and after she had ripped out his soul.

Day 61

My phone was gone. I threw it against a wall, against the ground.

I stood on it.

I smashed it into pieces as small as the confidence I had that everything would be alright.

It was a school day, but because of the curfew, no one was going.

No one was going anywhere.

Not known to anyone else, at least.

The entire town had gone into lockdown.

And I was cut off from everyone.

No phone.

No nothing.

I heard a knock at the door and everything exploded inside me. What was she doing here? Why was she here?

'Hello, Mrs Andrews.'

Glenn.

It was Glenn.

Always Glenn.

He was here to save me.

He would save me.

I heard Mum hesitate before letting him in, then I heard footsteps on the stairs.

Reminding me of her.

Footsteps on the stairs.

I had never heard them.

Glenn opened my bedroom door without knocking, then came and sat on the edge of the bed.

'Hey.'

'Hey.'

Silence.

'You're out?'

He nodded.

'I snuck out. Your mum let me in. Wants me to speak to you. My mum and dad were too busy talking about everything to even notice. You know what they're like. If it isn't something to do with keeping me here, they don't care.'

I nodded.

There was more he wanted to say.

'You heard about Archie.'

It wasn't a question.

'Yeah. Zara ... told me.'

Silence.

'It wasn't me,' Glenn said.

I looked at him, trying to hide my shock he would say that, saying nothing, then I nodded.

'I know.'

Still more.

He was holding something back.

But not for long.

'So I have been doing some research,' he said.

I rolled over. I didn't want to hear it, didn't want to hear anything. Research? On what? Small-town killings?

'On small-town killings.'

Oh, Jesus.

Glenn launched into telling me all about it, how these things happened, why people thought they happened, but it was a blur of words, of nothingness.

And then I heard a single word.

Zara.

I spun back, stared at him.

'What did you say?'

'What's happening. It's happened before. A girl gets bullied. The kids who bully her die, one by one. It's happened before.'

'Not here.'

'No, at other schools. Over and over again, at other schools, but never close enough to seem like it's the same thing.'

'I don't get it,' I said, and I didn't. I really didn't. What was he trying to tell me? She'd done this before? How did he even know it was her this time?

Her.

Me.

He didn't.

But he did.

'I'm not saying it's her, I don't get how it could have been her, but look.'

He held out a sheet he'd printed out. Newspaper articles, some sort of recent, some from years before.

Like, years before.

Twenty years ago, forty years ago, eighty years ago.

Articles about killings of schoolkids.

Photos of the deceased.

Photos of teachers, parents, funerals.

And at every funeral, in every photo, in amongst the hundreds of mourners, one face stood out.

Every time.

It was the face that stared out at me from the photo Glenn had of Sienna's funeral.

The face that had eyes that stared into your soul.

The face that had breathed life into me, had rested against mine, kissed me, loved me.

It was the face of the most beautiful person I had ever known, and it was the face of a killer, the face I knew was that of a killer, but I knew it from my time.

It was the face I had to see again, to find out the truth, and to put a stop to this.

'It's Zara,' Glenn said.

Well, yeah, I know that, Glenn! I mean, you can't read my thoughts, but seriously? It's kind of obvious.

'Or someone that looks a lot like her,' he said, trying to place reality into the frame, but I knew better.

I had lost reality a long time ago, as soon as she had looked around the room, as soon as I had been swept underwater at Sienna's, as soon as I had seen the blood on my hands. Reality was an illusion I didn't want and yet craved.

She was an illusion I didn't want and yet craved.

And, curfew or not, I had to see her.

Now.

I left the house. Glenn wanted to come with me, but I wouldn't let him.

'I have to see her alone,' I said.

He wouldn't let it go.

'Dude, it's her. I don't know how it's her, but it's her. She killed them. Not just Sienna, or Archie, or Ashleigh, she killed them *all*. Like *all* all.'

I shook my head.

'It's a coincidence. It has to be. People look like other people all the time.'

Glenn shook his head.

'No one looks like her. No one.'

He was right. It was her. It had to be her. But why? And how? And ... I thought something I didn't want to believe, but had to find out, so I grabbed the articles, I left Glenn in my room and I ran.

I would find her.

I always found her.

And I did again. I ran until I found it hard to breathe, and when I slowed down, near the park, I saw her there, watching me, playing with her scarf, her eyes, even from a distance, drawing me in, drawing me a masterpiece.

I went to her, but neither of us sprinted this time.

When we met though, when we were within reach, I couldn't hold back. I knew what she was and what she did, but I couldn't hold back.

I was in the whirlwind.

But now I was in control.

Now I needed to know.

I reached up and held her face in my hands, and then I kissed her, and when I broke off the kiss, when I looked at her, I slid my hand to her scarf.

She made a noise, a small whimper, but she didn't flinch.

Not one bit.

Because she knew.

She already knew what I wanted.

I wanted to see beneath the scarf, see what was there.

I needed to know something more than anyone else, and then, perhaps, I could ask her about the articles.

In the end, I didn't ask her anything.

I kissed her again, and the she pressed her forehead against mine, our mouths still together, but not kissing anymore, just there, breathing each other's breath, being with each other.

She moved my hand away, and I let her, and then I put it back, I had to see, I *had* to, and she tried to stop me again but I was stronger, I *was* stronger, I convinced myself of that, and without moving my forehead from hers, without opening my eyes, as ice filled the air, sleet, hail, thunder, as the wind rushed over us, threatening to sweep us away, as I was overwhelmed by pastel blues and greys, choking me, I tore the scarf from her neck.

I had said I wanted to see.

I had said I would do anything.

I had meant every single word, but when I opened my eyes, when the scarf was off, when there were no pastel blues and greys, when there was no *her*, when I was choking on the smell of death, when I saw her as she really was, all I could do was scream.

Day 62

I lay in bed, Glenn sitting on the edge of the bed.

'A monster?'

'Yes. No. I don't know, Glenn. I know what I saw and what I smelt, and I know her, but I know what I saw and what I smelt.'

'Like, scales and teeth and stuff?'

I almost laughed. Glenn was so small-town movie goer. Everything was Hollywood. But this wasn't. This wasn't make-up or effects or anything.

This was horror.

This was real.

I sat up and looked at him.

'I don't know what she is, but I know it was her. All those other times, it was her. And this time as well. But not just her, Glenn.'

He looked at me, then looked down.

'Did you really look at the photos?' he asked. I shook my head.

'You should look. And read the articles.'

He put them on the bed and stood.

'I gotta go, man. Look closer, okay?'

I nodded, and he left, and an hour later, when I finally worked up the courage, I picked up the first article, from 100 years ago, and I read it.

And the next one.

And the next, and the next, and the next.

And every time it was the same.

And every time, in the photo, with Zara, was a boy. A different boy each time, but a boy who was looking at her, lost in her, in desperate love with her.

And then the articles, articles about how the deaths had affected the other children, and how it had led to suicides, two every time, first a friend, a girl, and every time that girl was Zara, although she wasn't Zara, not by name, she was Annika, and she was Corinne, and she was Lily, and she was name and name and name, over and over, always a new name, always the same death, wrists slit, a blade, scissors, a knife, cut cut cut.

More articles, stories of the boy who had committed suicide after the funeral, after their girlfriend had left them alone to deal with everything.

And every boy was the one in the photo.

Every boy was the one who had been with Zara Annika Corinne Lily name name name, staring at her, lost in her, in desperate love with her.

And in the last photo, the most recent funeral photo, that boy looking at her was me.

Day 65

It was 11.25pm. We were still in lockdown. Still no school. No going out after 8:45pm now. The police were asking questions, kids were giving answers, parents were giving answers.

No one had spoken to me.

Not yet.

On Day 65, no one had asked me, and what would I say? 'It was me! I did it, and I would do it again, for her, because that's what she does! That's what she does to us! She lures us in, and she makes us kill for her, and then she leaves us and moves on. Sher leaves us devastated, and we have no other choice but to ...'

I had been there before, wanted to do it, to end it all, after Avril, and Zara had known that, had said she had been glad I didn't do it, but was she really?

Was she just glad because now it could be because of her, now she could lead me to the end?

Tap.

Tap.

Tap.

No.

Please no. Not now, not today, not ever again!

Tap.

Tap.

Tap.

I rolled over, pulled the covers over my head, blocked my ears, scrunched my eyes as tight as they would go, screamed into my pillow, muffling the sound, but still I heard tap ... tap ... tap.

'**GO AWAY!!!**' I screamed into the pillow. 'Please just go away, I don't want to die now, I don't want to. You have made me see there is life, and I don't want to die. Not yet.'

Tap.

Tap.

Tap.

I went to the window and threw it open, screaming into the freezing air outside, '*Come on then! Come on!*'

I looked down, but she wasn't there. In the darkness, on the lawn, there was no one looking up at me.

My shoulders dropped.

After it all, I had wanted her to be there, looking up, smiling, rocking my world.

I turned around and screamed, face to face with Zara, looking incredible, clear, pure, alive, real.

'**HUNTER?**'

Mum. On the stairs. I pushed Zara behind the door as I opened it, Mum almost crashing into me, hand raised to knock, throwing her arms around me now.

'Hunter, what is it, are you okay?'

I nodded into the hug, holding her close, giving her what she wanted so she would go.

'Sorry, Mum. I drifted off, had a dream, then thought I heard something outside.'

'And? What the hell, Hunter? What did you see?'

'It was nothing.'

'Nothing? You're shaking, your heart is racing, and you look like you've seen a ghost.'

I broke off the hug, not wanting her to see my face.

'It's okay, Mum, really. I'll come down in a bit if you want to have a coffee with me? I just need a minute.'

She stared at me for a moment and then nodded.

'Okay, Hunter, but we're doing this, okay? I'm not going to lose you.'

'I know, Mum. I know.'

She left and I closed the door, my hand resting on the handle before I turned around, and before I could she was there, holding me, and it was as though everything from Day 61 disappeared, and I was holding my Zara again, and I was breathing her in, and the skies were clear, and her hands were on my neck, and I could smell her, every perfect part of her, and when I leant back and looked at her, she had never looked more beautiful, and it was as though everything from Day 61 had disappeared.

But it hadn't.

It never would.

I pulled away from her and went and sat on the bed.

She walked over and sat next to me, knees not touching.

She played with her scarf with her left hand, with a thread on her dress with her right, as she spoke.

'I miss you, Hunter.'

I sucked in a breath. I missed her too. I missed us. I missed the bubble.

'It's almost over, you know,' she said, the thread curling around her perfect, icy finger. 'It's almost over.'

I knew what she meant. Only Julie and Marcus remained. The final two. They would not be spared. They couldn't be. I knew she couldn't rest now, maybe she couldn't rest at all until …

'They didn't commit suicide.'

'Hunter?'

Her face was pure innocence and beauty, her eyes pools of grey steel.

'The boys. At your other schools. They didn't commit suicide. You killed them.'

She looked away.

'Hunter, this has been a very hard time. For everyone. There have been a lot of deaths, and you …'

She turned back, and stared into me.

'You have been amazing. You have saved me, given me life. Hunter, without you I would have …'

Her voice trailed off again, only this time I knew what she

was saying. I had been her ray of light. I had done for her what I hadn't for Avril. I had been there and I had swum in the depths with her.

But now, now I was doubting her.

Because I had to.

'Did they know? Did they find out too?'

'Find out what, Hunter? Hunter, find out what? What boys? I have had boyfriends, yes, but none like you, Hunter. No one is like you.'

I searched her eyes, and could find only truth. And then I realised that she didn't know. She remembered the bullying, the torture, the schools, but that was it.

She was in a loop, an endless loop of the world tearing her down, and she didn't even remember the boys dying.

She didn't even remember ... she didn't know she was dead.

She only knew now, what was happening now, and so she would be stuck in the loop forever.

I moved to her, knees touching, and I grabbed her arms.

'I have to save you,' I said. 'I don't care about Julie, or Marcus. I don't care what I have to do to them. I have to save you. I have to free you. Tell me what to do, Zara. Please, tell me what to do!'

I was whisper shouting, not wanting to alert Mum, but wanting Zara to know how desperate I was to help her, how desperate I was to end her pain, because she was living in pain, endless, torturous pain, heaped on her because her clothes weren't right, because she was so smart, so amazing, and despite her energy, it was energy borne of decades of heartache, of lost loves, of solitude, of searching for the one who would save her.

Who would release her.

I would be her ray of light.

I would finish this.

I just had to find out how.

I hadn't gone down for coffee. I had meant to, but I didn't. I forgot. No. I didn't even think of it. I locked myself in my room. No one wanted us on the streets, out of the house.

I would take that to the extreme.

She stayed with me overnight, on Day 68. I had asked about her mum, if she knew she was out, if she knew she was with me, but she silenced me with a kiss, and at first, I resisted, I had to, I had seen ... her, and I didn't know if I could kiss that, if I could love that, but I loved *her*, I loved her with an ache and a desire that I could even see past what she was, I could even breathe her in, because while that scarf was on, she was Zara, my Zara, and she smelt like pastel blues and greys and she tasted like Summer and she felt like us.

She felt perfect.

So I let my resistance drop away, drip, drip, drip, raindrops on leaves after the storm, but I knew the storm was still here, I knew this was us taking shelter while it still raged outside, searching, destroying, regenerating, and then the storm was in us, and it filled us with passion like I had never known, and it was even better than on Day 39, it was death giving me life.

I lay with a killer of old, and I had never felt safer.

Afterwards, we held each other, stroking each other, and I asked her about Julie, about Marcus, and she said she hoped they would be okay, but we both knew they wouldn't be, there was still a charade, and I probed and I searched, and I needed to know more, so I could help her.

Save her.

Be with her.

But I also knew that if I helped her, if I released her from the loop, then I could never be with her, because I would be releasing her from this world, from me, from us.

I was torn.

But I knew she came first, she had to.

It was about saving her, regardless of what I lost.

If I was her ray of light, that was how it had to be.

I asked about her other schools, and she told me, talked to me, said what had happened, and it had been the same every time, the tests and the questions and the clothes and the Julies, whatever their names, and now that I knew, now that I knew what she was it started to make sense. The references she made, the language, it was new but old, modern but the past, and it proved to me what I knew was right.

She wasn't of this time.

She didn't quite fit in.

But she didn't know why.

She didn't realise.

She spoke about these schools as though they were all in the recent past.

'Last year was the worst,' she said. 'Last year they really turned it on with me, really pressed hard. Hunter. Last year was the worst.'

Only it wasn't last year.

The last killings had been 20 years before.

20 years that felt to her like yesterday.

She didn't know she was in the loop, didn't know that she was coming back at a certain time, and that she would keep coming back until ... something different happened.

Did she need to kill them all? Had she always ended it before then? Had her boyfriend died because he hadn't been able to help her, or because he had lost everything? Had any of them known, any of the boys, the Dales and Andrews and Marks and name name names?

Had they seen all of her?

Like I had seen all of her?

'Tell me what to do,' I said. 'Tell me. Let me save you. I can't let you end it, not on your own.'

She had looked at me, those grey eyes hardening slightly, and for a second I felt like I was next, that she would end me, that maybe she had ended the other boys, it hadn't been suicide, but she had gone first, how could it have been her, but she was here now, too, so maybe she ...

'Save me? Oh Hunter, you will be with me, all the way. When it ends, when the last drop of rain falls, when the rainbow appears, you will be with me. It's almost over, Hunter, we are so close now. Soon we'll be free.'

No, I thought. You think you will be, but you won't. You will never be free if the cycle stays the same.

And then I knew.

I knew what I had to do.

I had to do it for her, save her from killing them, save her soul. I could deal with it, I could be the ghost, in a loop, I could handle it, but she couldn't, not anymore, not the endless bullying, torture, this was it, this was going to be it for me, but I would take her place, it would be me, I would be her ray of light and she actually *would* be free.

And it would all start with Marcus.

That night, she came to me, and we went out. We broke the curfew we knew no one else would, not Marcus or Julie at least, they would be home, playing the perfect children as usual, keeping up the facade, always Julie.

Not us.

We weren't perfect, far from it, but we were perfect.

Together, we were perfect.

It would kill me for us to part, and it would kill me for us to part.

But so it was, and so it had to be.

We stood outside Marcus's house, looking at the windows, some dark, two lit up, people still awake. It was 10:37pm.

'That's his room,' Zara said, pointing to one of the rooms that had been lit up. 'He's there, awake. He's talking to Julie.'

I turned to her.

'How do you know?'

'I'm here with you, Hunter, always here with you, but I am there as well, in the room with him.'

Her hand found mine. She wouldn't look at me, didn't look at me, all her energy on the window.

'They're talking about me. About us,' she said. 'Talking about what they can do. They don't know, but they want someone else to hurt. She blames me. Says it has only started since I came. Like in her poem.'

'You loved that poem.'

'No. I love you.'

Now she looked at me, holding both my hands. I never felt the chill anymore, not like at the start, not when it had gone through my bones. Now we were one, now I was her and she was me, our temperature matched like we matched, perfectly, completely, fully.

'I love you, Hunter. It's like I always have, in some form, known I would be with you, known I would find you, known you would know me.'

I couldn't breathe. It wasn't me she knew she would meet, it was a boy who would love her. She was remembering the others, knowing they were there, not putting the pieces together, not realising, but I did, and it was okay, because now it was me.

She loved *me*.

She leaned in, her breath on my face, mouth, lips, hovering, so close I ached to move, not daring to, not wanting to but wanting to.

'Are you ready?' she asked. 'Are you ready for us to join. That's when it happens, you know. That's when another piece of me is set free. When we join.'

Every word she spoke made her lips brush against mine, not a kiss, but more intimate than I could believe possible. A noise escaped my lips, not a breath or a cry but a whimper, a sound of longing, of pleading, of desire and love, and still I held back, still, the minuscule gap remained, still every single cell in my being longed for her, but still I held back as she did, and then she moved closer, as impossible as that seemed, and still we didn't kiss, but the electricity was everywhere, and then thunder, lightning, lightning flashing into us, between us, into that tiny gap, scorching us, and then she pressed into me, first with her hips, and then with her lips, and I was gone, drowning, swirling, tossed and turned like seaweed in the ocean, sheets of rain powering into the surface of the water while I was rag-dolled underneath, and always she was there, never parting, our mouths connected our souls meshed, no, not meshed, our soul our soul, it wasn't two souls joined it was one that always had been and always would be, no matter what, and no matter what may be, and then we weren't alone, someone else was there, *why was someone else there, how* was someone else there, and then I saw him and it was Marcus and he was with us not with us, swishing side to side, head above water, the rain drenching his head, his body always swishing side to side, and then we were beside him, around him, holding his body between us, and he was facing her then facing me and I heard his voice, 'Oh her poor eyes, she wishes she couldn't watch,' and I heard that over and over and over again and as I heard it his face changed from the peacefulness of sleep to the the sneering, animal-like face he'd had as the books were destroyed in front of her me us we, and I saw that face and my entire body filled with rage, pure, white hatred, and I let go of her hands, I let go of her, but still she held me, somehow, and somehow her hands guided me but I didn't need it, I knew this was it, what I had to do, and I reached up and I stabbed my thumbs into Marcus's eyes and I pressed, I pressed so hard everything good in me hurt and still I pressed, through the pain, through the knowledge of what I was doing, this wasn't me waking up from a dream into a life of knowing, this was me in full awareness of what I was doing and still his body swayed side to side, and still I pressed, even harder now, feeling the squelch as the eyeballs were pressed further back, squelch squish, stress balls, that was what popped into my mind, I was pressing two stress balls and I laughed, I laughed and I pressed and black blood seeped around my thumbs, not washed away because there was no water, and still he swayed side to side, and I tore my thumbs away, and as I did I ripped what remained of his eyes from their sockets and then she was there with me and she held me and we left him, alive, and we were back on the lawn again, holding each other, my thumbs holding the remnants of all Marcus would ever see, and still he swayed, side to side.

And now, all that remained was Julie.

Always Julie.

Day 74

For five days, the police pressed harder. Not only were we confined to our homes, not only was there no school, not only did security and police now patrol the streets every hour of every day, it would all continue until the attacker was found, until they could assure the parents that their children were safe.

They were blinder than Marcus. Not one attack had occurred outside. Not one. We were safer outside. In our houses, we were vulnerable, our comfort zone our deathbed.

Not our.

Them.

"They."

And now only Julie remained.

Only Julie.

On Day 74, late at night, Zara came to me. We didn't say a word. We just held each other. I was protecting her, but she was somehow protecting me too, her scarf a shield for us both, and no one suspected me of anything, and I suddenly realised she had said it about her, but it was about me as well.

I was never a suspect because I was always somewhere else.

I had never "been" at Ashleigh's, or Tracey's, or Marcus's. Not really.

'I am always with you, even when I am there.'

She had taken me there, never letting go of my hand, never

losing connection because to do so would be to send me back to myself, back to my room, to McDonalds.

And now only Julie remained.

Always Julie.

It would be tonight, I knew it would be.

It had to be.

It was Day 74, and in all the articles, in everything I read of her past, it had been Day 74. Talking of her suicide, the other kids had talked about the day she had arrived, how she had changed them, how she had been like a cool breeze on a Summer day, and how it was a great loss now that she was gone. These kids who had tortured her, pushed her to the edge, been a part of her destruction, they said these things.

I took her hands in mine.

'Let me feel the cold,' I said. 'One more time. Let me feel it.'

She smiled, and a rush of ice surged through me, and I gasped and then I relaxed, breathed into it, into the ice, the cold, and then the cold turned to heat, and my body flushed red, and then I was back to normal, to a perfect temperature, and I didn't know if that was hot or cold or normal, and it didn't matter, I wasn't a temperature, I was a feeling, and I was perfect.

'I'm ready,' I said. 'I'm ready to end this.'

She didn't say a word.

She nodded, and she hugged me, and then we were on Julie's lawn, outside her house, one first floor light on, otherwise the house silent, still, waiting.

Filled with life.

For now.

'Hunter?'

Her voice was low, almost scared, and now I did feel a chill. I needed her to be as strong as me.

Stronger.

Better.

'This is where it ends, Hunter. After this, I don't know. I don't know what happens after tonight.'

I did, but I couldn't tell her. This was where her memories ended, this night, with her death, her suicide, something she thought would set her free but which only imprisoned her.

Not tonight.

First Julie.

Always Julie.

Then me.

Then, and only then, could she be free.

'It doesn't matter,' I said. 'What happens after tonight doesn't matter, because of everything that has happened before. Every moment since the time you walked into the room, from the time you looked up, from the time I first saw these eyes, smelt your pastel blues and greys, every moment has been building to now and the after will happen, and it will build to something else, and then we will be somewhere saying what will happen next, and I won't care. Because I will have had the moments before.'

She kissed me, hard but soft, passionately but gently, full of desire but full of restraint, and then she let herself go and this time she lost herself in *me, she* drowned in *me*, and we went into Julie's house to finish everything.

Julie was in her bath. Lying there, naked, eyes closed, music playing softly. We watched her for a moment, both of us, standing there, holding hands, invisible to her, and then her words found me.

'I hope this hurts you everywhere, and that the pain never stops.'

This was not going to be quick, or clean. This was rusty blade slow death, if death was ever reached.

We took a step and then the unthinkable happened.

'I knew you would come.'

Julie.

Always Julie.

'How do you know?' Zara whispered, and again I felt the fear in her, and I squeezed her hand. Not tonight, Zara. Tonight you are free. Tonight I am the strong one, for you, for you have been so strong, always, and tonight I set you free.

Julie's eyes snapped opened and she looked at us, only she didn't look at us. She could sense us, feel us, but she couldn't see us.

The music played.

'Oh, Hunter's the only one who can read? Hunter's the only one who can look up articles? Hunter's the only one who has a friend?'

Glenn.

Glenn?

'He won't be your friend anymore, Hunter. He won't be anyone's friend.'

No. Not Glenn.

'What did you do?' I hissed.

'Nothing worse compared to anything you two have done ... or maybe it was. Or maybe it's the same, it doesn't matter. Glenn's gone.'

'You killed him.'

Julie searched for us, trying to find us, find where the voices were, but we remained invisible.

'Let me see you,' she spat. 'Let me see you, cowards!'

Zara's grip on my hand weakened, but I pulled her back. We had to stay connected. We had to be we.

I turned to her.

'I'm not letting you go,' I said. 'I won't.'

'Awwww, so stupid and sweet,' Julie said, standing up, but I didn't move, I couldn't look away from Zara, from her eyes, flashing grey and blue, the steel of death gone, the doubt returning.

'I don't remember,' she whispered. 'I don't know what happens next.'

She was losing control.

Waves crashing, sheets of rain, thunder overhead, life draining away.

I turned back to Julie, still holding Zara's hand, but before

I could do anything Julie shoved her, hard, and she was ripped away from me, the connection broken, and I was back in my room, standing in exactly the same spot I had been before we left.

But I was alone.

Day 75

It was Day 74, but it was Day 75, midnight having just been passed as I passed the park where Zara had kissed me, leaving me on the swing, watching her leave.

I had run, in the past, until my throat burned and my legs screamed at me to stop, but now I was deaf to all screams.

I was deaf to all burning.

I was deaf to everything except the thought that ran through my mind, over and over again.

You are her ray of light.

Will you let it end this way?

HELL.

NO.

And so I ran.

Julie's house wasn't far from mine, but it was far enough, when I was running in the street, in the darkness, and she was there with Zara, in the light.

Here, there, place had no meaning except we weren't in the same one.

And so I ran.

I didn't know if I would be too late, and I didn't know what I would be too late for.

And so I ran.

I knew that she was my everything. She had come to me, and I had seen her, and I knew her, and I needed her.

And so I ran.

And I ran.

And I ran.

When I arrived at Julie's I ran over her lawn, picking up a

gnome as I did. Before I reached the window of the bathroom, the only room with a light on, I hurled the gnome, smashing it against the glass, smashing the glass enough for me to dive shoulder-first into it, crashing through, rolling on the ground, broken glass stabbing me a thousand times, but I was deaf to it.

I stood immediately, and then I saw it.

Just like before.

Just like always.

Zara Annika Corinne Lily name name name in the bath, still clothed, scarf still on, sleeves rolled up, the storm raining blood into the water, wrists slit, only "they" were wrong, every other time "they" were wrong, it hadn't been suicide, it hadn't been her who had finally finished it, she hadn't been able to set herself free, she never *had* been able to because it had been Julie, always Julie, standing there, a knife in her hand, blood dripping from the end, and I didn't know how she had done it, I didn't know if it was because we had lost our connection, if it was because I had left her alone, all I knew was that this wasn't how it ended.

This wasn't how *she* ended.

How the loop ended.

'Hunter, I remember this now.'

This was our story, our love, our time.

Julie stared at me. She was frozen in time, the knife in her hand, blood dripping onto her leg as she raised it towards me.

'No, Hunter, you shouldn't be here. You can't know this.'

Had the other boys committed suicide as well?

I knew the answer.

I *was* the answer.

This time.

Julie lunged at me, the water still on her skin spattering against me in slow motion as the knife glanced the hand I put up to defend myself. I backed away as she slashed again, wanting to end this, but she missed, and I was deaf to the pain in my hand, but not to Zara.

'Hunter.'

She gave me strength. She was my strength. She was me. I rolled from another lunge, glass stabbing me, staying in me like she stayed in me, like she would stay in me until the end.

As I stood Julie was on me, the blade sinking into my chest at my shoulder, and I bit back a scream and shoved her off me. She grunted as she hit the ground and was up in an instant, coming back at me but I was ready this time, and the shard of glass I held found its target, slashing down her arm, but she found the target as well, and this wasn't like when I was with Zara, it wasn't, this was raw, this was real, this was Zara in the bath, too weak to stand even, the blood draining from her.

HELL.

NO.

Julie had stumbled and I slashed again, the glass cutting my own hand as I sliced her collarbone. She jumped at me and I thrust, and the glass buried into her shoulder, but the other end of it stabbed through my hand and for an instant we were joined, and wasn't a connection, but it held us there and she stabbed me again in the shoulder, aiming for my heart, and still my hand was jammed on her, but it was perfect and I used my free hand to punch with all my might, hitting Julie square on the jaw, separating us and sending her backwards, her head smashing the side of the bath, her knife still in me, Julie on the ground, broken glass entering her body, her neck, blood flowing from her head.

I spun to Zara, kneeling by the bath, lifting her head and cradling it in my hands.

'Hunter.'

'You can't. You can't leave me. This isn't how it ends. You'll just come back. *This isn't how it ends!*'

She sucked in a breath, and I could feel her weakening.

'It is, Hunter. I remember now. This is what happens, every time. This is how it ends.'

'*This* is why you always come back. *This* is why you can never be free. We have to change it, and there's only one way.'

She knew. She always knew. When we were together,

when we were connected, she always knew my thoughts, and even though she was weakening, even though the blood still flowed, taking her away from me, but it wouldn't be me next time, it wouldn't be me, it *had* to be me.

'No, Hunter. This is how it ends.'

'Not this time.'

We stared at each other, her eyes back to the way they were the first time I had seen them, the most beautiful blue in the world, the most beautiful anything anywhere, the most her, and suddenly, against the pain, she rocked my world, and all I could do was cry against her smile.

'It seems,' she whispered to me, 'that we are at an impasse.'

I sobbed into her shoulder, her arm around me now, holding me and I could feel her weakening, and then suddenly she pushed me away and she stood, and from the ground I felt rather then saw Julie come at me, and I felt the blade being wrenched out of my shoulder, and then she lunged again, and this time she wouldn't miss, she couldn't, I was open, it was over, the loop would continue.

But the knife didn't hit home.

Julie's wrist was grabbed, as it had been so long ago in class, only this time it was grabbed with such force I heard and saw the bones crack.

No. Not crack. Shatter.

I looked up. Zara had a hold of Julie, and as we looked up at her, as she twisted Julie's arm, lifting her to her feet, as she did that, her eyes went the purest black.

'Do you remember the last time I grabbed you, Julie?' she asked. 'You tried to see under the scarf. Do you remember?'

Julie squirmed, trying to get away from the pain, unable to as Zara lifted her higher.

'Well look now, Julie. Look now, because I want to give you everything you deserve.'

And with that she reached up, an she took off her scarf, and Julie screamed from the depths of everything, and as she did,

Zara ripped the arm clean off her body.

'Pain, Julie. This will hurt you everywhere, and the pain will never stop.'

Julie scrambled backwards, and Zara stepped out of the bath, strong again, and she reached down and she wrenched Julie's other arm off, and I pressed back against the wall, away from Julie's scream, and then Zara reached down and grabbed Julie by the mouth, and with a sickening crack she broke her jaw, and then she did it, the pain did stop, she stopped the pain, she drove her hand inside of Julie, reaching into her and ripping out her heart.

Julie.

Always Julie.

Not any more.

Zara stood over her for a while, and then she took her scarf and placed it back around her neck, and as soon as she did, she collapsed again, onto me, her human form unable to cope with the loss of blood.

I held her close, rocking her.

'It has to be me,' I said. 'You changed the ending. You saved me, you killed Julie this time, but to end the loop, I have to go first. It has to be me. It's the only way it can end. The only way we can be together. You can't feel like you left me here alone, and I can't find you if you go first. It has to be me. And you have to do it.'

She mumbled something into my neck, something, anything, it didn't matter, I was deaf to anything, deaf to everything except the touch of her on me, and then she raised her head a little, and she looked at me, eyes so blue they looked like they had been painted on.

'Do you remember what you asked me on Day 9?'

I remembered.

'Why do you wear that scarf every day? And why -'

'So I could find you, Hunter. So I could find you. You are my hero. You are my ray of light, and now, we will always be together. Always.'

She kissed me, and we were underwater again, only this time the water was perfect, still, and it held us, it held us as the glass slid painlessly down my arms, it held us as the glass sliced through my skin, my veins, and it held us as the blood seeped from my body, from hers, from ours, from we, and it held us as the life seeped from my body, from hers, from ours, from we, and at the end, right at the very end, she took off her scarf, and she wasn't the monster, but she wasn't Zara either, not exactly, she was she as she had been at the start, the first time, the first round of the loop, and she was the most beautiful thing I had ever seen.

She had arrived like the afternoon wind on a Summer day, cooling the heat that had held us captive. She touched us so gently at the start that we didn't even realise it was happening, and then, by the end, she was a presence none of us could ignore, a gale force, a whirlwind, tearing through us like we were paper.

She changed everything.

She changed everyone.

She changed me.

ABOUT THE AUTHOR

Zara is Marcus Hamilton's debut novel, and the first of many he hopes to publish with Krueger Wallace Press.

Marcus completed a professional writing degree before working as a teacher, where his experiences led him to write a short story about a girl stuck in a loop.

That story became Zara.

Marcus now lives in Ivanhoe East, where he writes every day and takes walks by the Yarra with his dog, Bear.